The Game Evil Plays

The Game Evil Plays

By
R. L. Stover

Strategic Book Publishing and Rights Co.

Copyright © 2014 R. L. Stover. All rights reserved.

No part of this book may be reproduced or transmitted in any form or by any means, graphic, electronic, or mechanical, including photocopying, recording, taping, or by any information storage retrieval system, without the permission, in writing, of the publisher.

Strategic Book Publishing and Rights Co.
12620 FM 1960, Suite A4-507
Houston, TX 77065
www.sbpra.com

ISBN: 978-1-62857-281-0

DEDICATED TO

MOM–Thank you for all the love and support you gave me. I wouldn't be who I am without you.

DAD–Thank you for being the man you didn't have to be.

BANDIT–My old friend. I miss you. Oh, the adventures we had together.

ACKNOWLEDGEMENTS

THIS HAS BEEN an exciting and fulfilling journey for me. It has been a goal of mine to write a book and tell my tale. My life was as depicted in the early goings of this story.

I would like to thank some people who have supported and helped me along the way.

Dustin Strayer, Frank Williams, and John Rogers are associated with the Dale Carnegie training courses. "If it is to be ... it is up to me" are the ten most powerful words in the English language. Thank you to the Dale Carnegie instructors who helped me reach inside myself to strengthen my confidence to obtain my full potential.

Thank you to my co-workers who provided me with encouragement and helped to keep me positive through the long and, at times, trying road: Darren, Donnie, Holly, Brad, Anthony, Joyce, Bruce, Nicole, Troy, Adam, Tim, Tami, and everyone else. A special thank you to Tami. She read along as I wrote to ensure my thoughts made it to paper correctly. Tami also helped with the title, which I feel is an accurate description of the book.

To all my Krazy Monkey Karaoke family: you are the best! Troy, Cori, Mike, Amy, John, Sheila, Joe, Kandis, Skippy, and Linda, thank you for all the good times, singing and hanging out. All of you filled me with confidence at times when I doubted the success of this project.

Tommy and Pam: Your encouragement and sincerity has meant the world to me. Thank you for always being there for me and for all you have said to keep me pushing through. The excitement you displayed was pure and honest and I will never forget that.

To my family: I wouldn't trade one minute of my life that was spent with you for anything. Mom, Dad, Matt, Leslie, Te'a, Lili, and Grandma, you all have taught me courage, love, and the true meaning of family.

Devon and Donavon: I am so proud of the men you two have become. One day you will understand that feeling when you have your own children. Remember, your actions always speak louder than your words.

Finally, to my love, Steph: I love you! Thank you for the patience you showed while I was writing this tale. I spent many hours siting and typing...deleting and retyping, and you supported me with every keystroke. This would not have been possible without you. XOXO

TABLE OF CONTENTS

In the Beginning 1
Moving In 10
The House 14
A New Friend 42
History – The Stevenson Games 48
Awareness 123
The First Move 132
The Game 135
The End Game 144
The Cross 158
Checkmate: The Game Evil Plays 161

IN THE BEGINNING

It was a beautiful June afternoon when Rob first saw the new house his mother, Mary, and his stepfather, Donnie, had just purchased. The sun was shining bright and a light breeze tickled the leaves as branches swayed from the warm winds. Rob had never heard his mother talk with such anxious excitement as she did when she talked about the house.

"Oh, Robbie, I can't wait for you to see our new home."

She must have said it a hundred times, or so it seemed to him. "After all we have been through, it seems that good fortune has finally decided to come our way."

She would go on and on. Rob loved to see her this way.

Mary was a hardened woman from years of disappointment and sorrow, or rather, she had grown cautious, not hardened. She was loving and kind. She was a true religious woman, with a family that strongly believed in the Lord. She wasn't easily fooled by the rhetorical talk that men liked to throw at her. Actions. Actions were what she judged all people by. She often told Robbie, whom she affectionately called *him*, "Your actions will speak louder of your character as a man than any word will ever do. People and God are watching what you do, so choose your course carefully, sweetie, for we all reap what we sow."

She had raised Robbie on her own after she divorced his father, Mark, when Robbie was just two-years-old. There were many hard times after that, both emotionally and financially. Mary worked as a waitress at a local restaurant and Robbie spent most nights with a babysitter or at the restaurant. Mary worked to give all she could to her son, whom she loved with every ounce of her soul. All mothers have a special love and connection to their sons, and Mary ensured that Robbie and Matt, once he was born, never doubted her love. Although she couldn't afford to provide all the material things that most children his age had, Robbie had love, caring, and an understanding of life that took the place of those useless possessions, easily.

However, once Mary met Donnie Silver, the hard times disappeared and life began to change for Robbie and her. She was able to feel the love of a man that was honest and dependable. Rob had a man, a real man, in his life now. Donnie enjoyed talking to him and spending time with him. He did just about anything with Rob. Rob and Donnie played games together on the Atari, and they went outside and played ball. Sometimes they just sat and talked about how school was or anything else that happened to come up. It really struck Rob when they played word search puzzles together. It wasn't very exciting, but Rob really enjoyed spending time with a father figure. Hunting for words together was something he had needed for a very long time (well, a long time to him, anyway). That honestly built a relationship that could never be destroyed. Donnie was being the man he didn't have to be, he was being the man Mary, Robbie, and Matthew, Robbie's younger brother, who was just two at the time, had needed and had prayed for so many nights.

Donnie was a tall man, or at least he was to Robbie. Mark was only five foot eight, so Donnie's six foot one frame was big to him. He had dark hair and dark eyes, with an athletic build. Not at all muscle bound, but he was defined from years of labor jobs. Donnie was divorced too and was looking for love and a second chance at happiness. He didn't have kids of his own and was now about to take on not only a wife, but her two kids as well, which was a huge step for anyone. Any parent knows the tribulations they sometimes experience with children, but to step in and become a role model, after the process of maturing has started, is something quite different. Donnie was more than willing to take this challenge head-on. He hoped to build a family through trust, honesty, and love.

So Mary and Donnie decided to take the chance and get married. A few short months later, Mary was pregnant and there was the need for a bigger place to live. Currently, they resided in a small three bedroom, low-income apartment.

House shopping was slow and meticulous. The couple wanted a nice house where a family could grow, in a nice area with good schools. Then one day all the excitement started. They found a great home, with plenty of space and room to expand. There was an open yard all fenced in, with woods on two sides and a farm on the other. It was located in a nice school district too. So the paperwork was completed and the dream house was ready for the Silver family to move in.

For Rob, it was another move in his relatively short life of ten years. From what he could remember, he and his mother had relocated four different times. So the move wasn't as traumatic for him as it would be for most children. He was used to switching schools, making new friends, and exploring new areas. He was a pro at this sort of thing. He was happy and looked forward to starting a new life, filled with adventure and new experiences. He had not seen his new home yet but felt as though he had been there countless times through his mother's words.

"It's so beautiful, Robbie," she would say. "It just feels so homey, and you are going to love the area and the yard. Oh, my, are you ever going to love the yard." She said this with the love and excitement only a formerly single mother could express.

Mary was on cloud nine and, because of this, Robbie loved Donnie even more. Before Donnie came around, she always did her best to hide the depression she felt on a constant basis. She was the most unselfish person Robbie knew and not just because she was his mother. She wanted so much for her boys and tried so hard to be both a mother and a father, because a boy needs both, you know. Rob's father was in and out of his life, basically when it suited him. When he was in, he acted like he had always been there. This made it worse. When he was out... Well, he was out. He used to make idle promises he never kept. Mary knew his ways, but his son... Rob continued to believe that one day his father would grow to love him as much as Robbie did. But that day never came. The day Robbie learned this hard fact was a day that started with such childhood excitement and zest, it seemed destined to fail.

***

Robbie hardly slept the night before, because his father called and said he was going to pick him up in the morning for a full day of fun. Robbie didn't care what they did, he just loved his father so much and wanted so desperately to feel the love returned from the man whose name he bared. Mary was cautious with this situation. She knew of the lies

Mark told all too well. She tried to get Robbie to calm down so he could sleep.

"Honey, if you don't sleep you will not have the strength and energy to enjoy your day," Mary suggested in that motherly tone.

"Oh, Mom, trust me, I will have plenty of both," Robbie disagreed playfully.

"Well, Robbie, please keep in mind that he may not show up. I'm not trying to be mean, but I want you to be ready for that if it happens. He is not good at living up to his promises," she said with a heavy heart.

Breaking her son's heart was something she swore never to do, but she needed to protect him against one as well.

With a smile and a wink, Robbie retorted, "Not this time, Mom. Dad sounded so excited too! I know he will come. I just know it!"

***

So that morning Mary got up and got her giddy boy showered and dressed. She made him breakfast, which he poked at and barely ate because his tummy was completely full of butterflies. Robbie pulled a chair up to the window of the apartment that looked out over the front of the building. From this second-floor view, Robbie could see the road to the right, which pulled into the parking lot that led to the sidewalk. This route would bring his dad to him, waiting right at the open door with a hearty, loving smile and a powerful hug.

Morning turned into afternoon, and Robbie was still standing on the chair he had strategically positioned by the front window. He was still full of hope that his dad had worked late and overslept. *Wait... Was that his car?... Nope...*

There's another... Not him either... He is coming any moment, I know it, Robbie thought.

"Sweetie, come down from the chair and eat some lunch. I have a peanut butter and jelly sandwich, with some tomato soup ready for you," broken-hearted Mary said.

"Mom, if I come over there I won't see him coming and I won't be ready for him at the door. Plus, I am sure he is going to take me out to eat," Robbie said in an attempt to convince himself.

"Well, at least eat half the sandwich, sweetheart. You need something to eat. You barely touched your breakfast," Mary implored.

What kind of man does this to his son? It is one thing to lie to me, but to lie to Robbie and break his precious little heart is too much, that prick! she thought to herself as she smiled at her precious son.

"OK, Mom, if I can eat it over here so I don't miss him, then I will eat half," Robbie conceded.

Mary smiled and delivered half the sandwich to her son, with some milk that she placed on the window ledge. Robbie devoured the treat and drank the milk in a couple of loud gulping sounds.

The afternoon was quickly disappearing and there was till no sign of Father.

"He *is* coming, Mom," Robbie persisted. However, his mind was overpowering his heart and tears were building behind his blue eyes, blue eyes like his dad's. Robbie tried to hide his tears from his mother. Not because she would ever even think of the words "I told you so," but because it would mean he had lost hope.

"Come here, baby, and sit with Mommy," Mary solemnly requested.

"OK, Mommy," Robbie said. He gave into the emotion that had overtaken his soul, and he cried and felt a pain so deep in his soul he doubted it would ever stop hurting. Ever.

He climbed up on his mother's lap and she held him so tight. She comforted him while they both cried. He cried for the pain of feeling unloved and forgotten by the man he looked to as his hero. She cried, for she felt the childhood innocence leaving her little five-year-old angel. She cried because she felt somehow responsible, as if she could have prevented this from taking place. She attempted to take his pain, his sorrow and replace the dark with light. They both continued to cry and cry...

"Why, Mommy, why would Daddy not come after he said he would? Why would he not call me? Why does Daddy not love me anymore?" This was the question she knew would come but had prayed that it wouldn't. "What did I do wrong? What did I do to Daddy to make him not love me?" he said through tears and sobs of broken-hearted pain.

Mary cried out. She cried out for the words that she heard, that must have been there, building like wildfire in her young man's soul. *How do I explain this? How do I get him to understand life at such a young age?* she thought through her anguish and anger.

"Baby, I want you to look at me," she said softly. She had collected her thoughts, but her voice was still shaky.

Robbie pulled his head from her neck, where he was trying to hide his guilt and sadness. And as he looked at her, he could see her pain. "I am sorry I made you cry too, Mommy." He sounded perfectly innocent, like a boy who thought he had done something wrong. A boy who would never think of making anyone feel bad, especially not his mother.

"Baby, these tears are *for* you, not *because* of you. Please understand that, first of all. You know that Mommy loves you more than anything in the world, right?" she inquired.

"Of course, Mommy. I just wish Daddy loved me that much too is all." All the weight of the world seemed to rest on his throat.

"Honey, Daddy does love you. I don't know why he didn't come, but I do know that it had absolutely nothing to do with anything you did or said to him. You have done nothing wrong, *nothing*. Unfortunately, Dad just doesn't see love like we do," she explained.

"How can I help him see my love? How can I help him see love like we do?" he asked his mother.

"Sometimes we cannot get those we love to see things the way we would like them to. All we can do is show our love and hope for the best, but, sweetheart, we have to prepare ourselves for the worst," she said. "You have to be you, all the time. Don't ever change *you* for someone else, even for Dad. One day he will see you for the man you are becoming and will be."

Good Lord, why do I have to do this? Why does he have to grow up so fast? she thought to herself.

"Do you understand, sweetie?" she asked carefully.

"I guess, Mommy. It just hurts so bad." Robbie placed his head back onto her shoulder. Mary felt fresh tears on her skin and new sobs in her ear.

Not another word was said that night about Daddy. Robbie eventually settled down and sat on his mother's lap, rocking in the chair. Then a song came on that defined the young boy's childhood to his mother. It was "The Rose" by Bette Midler. Mary sang this song to him with the voice of an angel as far as Robbie was concerned. As she sang

"The Rose," Robbie started to understand the difference between unconditional love and love itself. What a thing to go through at five. He knew his mother would love him forever, no matter what, and while, yes, his father may love him, that love had conditions. It had boundaries, and those boundaries were put there by his dad.

MOVING IN

SO THE MORNING came for Mary to share her exhilaration with her son, and Robbie didn't let his mother down. He was excited and smiling from ear to ear, fidgety like a child on Christmas Eve. Mary seemed to float that morning, getting boxes together and just talking and talking about the new house, new hopes, a new future, and the new family.

Marie arrived at the apartment not a moment too soon. Marie, Donnie's mother, was a neat and proper woman. She enjoyed laughing and playing card games. Marie was always ready to spend time with Robbie and seemed to thoroughly enjoy his company. He was, of course, her first grandson, so to speak, and treated him as such. Henry, Donnie's father, was not there that morning, but Robbie really liked him and was looking forward to Donnie joining the group at the Stone House, as the new house was affectionately referred to.

The three of them, Mary, Marie, and Robbie, loaded the car with cleaning supplies and some kitchen appliances. Matt was strapped in his car seat next to Robbie and the journey to the Stone House began. On the way there, Robbie's anxiousness began to take root. He had heard so much of not just the house, but what the house represented to his mother. He could not wait to get started down the path of their new beginning.

As they got closer, his mom said, "Robbie, look, there's the raceway and the old stone bridge over the creek."

"Are we close, Mom? Because I can't wait to see the house," he asked, brimming with ten-year-old anxiousness.

She turned left off the main road, then made an immediate right. "Yep, honey, it's right there." She pointed forward, to the left of the windshield.

To the left of Robbie was an old, rundown country store. The store gave Robbie images of the old stores seen in western movies starring The Duke. John Wayne entertained Robbie on more than just a couple occasions. Six tall windows marked the front bottom portion of the store, with a glass door in the middle set back from the front wall. The building was tall, and Robbie was sure at one point that store must have been a very popular place. A sign on the front said "Willie's EST. 1875."

Just ahead was a tall oak tree which was standing strong in a grassy area that formed a triangle, with the side road on the right side, the church to the backside, and the stone driveway to the house on the left side. To the left of the stone driveway there was a big, old-looking garage that badly needed the wood replaced and a fresh coat of white paint. Robbie envisioned himself portraying Tom Sawyer, whitewashing that structure, which provided a slight grin of amusement on his youthful face. This faded slightly when he noticed the wood fence attached to the right front corner of the garage. It proceeded straight along the driveway to the far right hand corner of the property line for about 100 yards. The fence consisted of four wood planks running horizontally with the ground, each plank placed approximately six inches apart from the one below it. These planks were about six inches wide and were attached to square wooden posts about ten feet apart. Now it seemed as though countless days of his summer would consist of finishing such a task, but still he smiled because he did enjoy that type of chore.

Just a bit farther ahead, sitting about forty yards behind the small brick church, was another smaller brick building that was overgrown with weeds and thick vines from the woods. Robbie asked his mother what that building was, and as she stopped the car she replied, "That is an authentic one-room schoolhouse from the old days. This area, including the store back there, the church, the school, and even our new home are all part of a historical site. That's neat, I think, but you need to promise to stay out of the school, because it is old and dangerous to play around, OK?"

"Yes, Mom, I will stay away from there, I promise," Robbie said with a boyish charm that might have bordered on mischievousness.

"OK, good," she replied knowingly. "Now, let's get out so you can see our new home." She wanted him to start exploring, and she knew he really wanted to as well.

Robbie exited the car from the right, the side that was closest to the church. While sitting in the car he wasn't able to get a good view of the house. Once he was out of the car, he got his first real glimpse of their dream home. That boyish excitement went away, actually, it ran away, like one of those dumb blondes in a horror movie who didn't believe what was going on until it was chasing her down. The Stone House was seemingly glaring at him. He was caught in a trance, staring at the two windows sitting just above a level porch roof, and he swore the house was staring at him. His mother asked, "So what do you think?"

Before he could think of an appropriate response, he haphazardly responded, "I don't like it, it doesn't feel right... It scares me."

Sorrow filled Mary's heart and her shoulders dropped a bit. She had obviously hoped for a drastically different response. "Oh, Robbie, it's a beautiful house and there's nothing scary about it. I have been inside a number of times and have never felt more comfortable in a home before. Please, give it a chance. Just wait till you see the inside."

"OK, Mom, I'm sorry. Those windows up there just caught me off guard, I guess."

THE HOUSE

✦

THE *STONE HOUSE* loomed in front of him. Robbie didn't know why he felt the way he did, but he definitely knew he didn't like it. He grabbed a box of cleaning supplies and followed his mom through the wood gate at the end of the sidewalk. The sidewalk ran along the side of and passed the front of the house and over to two smaller buildings that looked like storage sheds. These buildings were newer and looked better than the fence and the garage. As he walked closer to the house, he realized this was the first time he had ever been that close to a real stone house. The stones varied in size and were held together by a half an inch of concrete. The walls of the house were not smooth like that of his apartment or the walls of Henry and Marie's house, which was brick. Although the wall seemed to be straight and solid, it wasn't flush and smooth. He reached out and touched the stone and, even though it was a warm summer day, the stone was cold, eerily cold. Robbie immediately pulled his hand back.

The side which faced the driveway had a door to the left and a big window to the right. Not a bay window by any means, but bigger than normal size. Here the sidewalk connected to the porch about twenty feet from the gate. The side of the house that faced the huge front yard had no windows, just solid rock and concrete. This was where the house seemed to have been built from its originally form. The stone portion of the house was a strong two-story building, which looked as if it stood the tests of time. At the end of the stone wall, the building set back a bit where there was another overhang to provide shade for the side of the house. There, to the right, was a door to go inside, and to the left were two metal doors which could be pulled up to gain access to the cellar. Farther to the left, along the side of the house, was a raised concrete slab where the cistern was located. Just to the left of that were three steps which led to the side yard and a sliding glass door for entrance into the newest portion of the house.

As Robbie checked out this side of the house, his mom was so excited she fumbled with the keys. She finally grasped control of herself enough to open the door. "Here we go!" she exclaimed, and the group walked through the doorway into the Stone House.

The door led into the dining room, which was about fifteen feet wide and twelve feet deep. Older grayish carpet covered the floor and the walls were painted a flat white. To the right was a doorway which led to the stone portion of the house. The door that guarded this entrance was thick and heavy oak, much bigger than any door Robbie had ever seen. From his standing position inside the dining room, he saw a flight of wood stairs leading to the second floor. They were along the left side of the wall, with a wood railing that connected to the ceiling of the room. To the left, which was where the rest of the party had gone, was a step to a small two-foot platform to gain access to the kitchen.

"Robbie, bring your box in here, please," his mother requested.

He entered the kitchen and sat his box on the standard modern-style counter. The kitchen was nice. It was big enough for a small table and fridge, with plenty of extra room to walk around in. Cupboards took over two sections of the walls, except for the space normally provided for the counter top and the sink. The walls, which were not obstructed by all the cupboard space, were covered with flowery wallpaper. To the back of the kitchen was a door, which was open, showing an old cast iron bathtub.

"OK, quick tour of the downstairs," Mary announced with exuberance. "Obviously, this is the kitchen, and just look at all the cupboard space. Where we walked in is actually the front door. We won't be using the door on the side that faces the driveway." She pointed to the dining room and proclaimed it as such. "Right there is the full bathroom, and just look at that wonderful old bathtub. I've always wanted a tub like that."

Robbie was listening intently to his mother, but he couldn't seem to take his eyes off her as she talked. *She is so happy and filled with so much energy*, he thought to himself. He smile caught Mary's attention. "I see you are warming up to the place, sweetheart."

"Well, actually, Mommy, I can see how beautifully happy you are and that makes me glad, but the house does seem very nice, too."

Mary's heart leaped with joy and she reached down and hugged her little man with all the love she could muster, which, for him, was more than most would ever feel, and at ten even Robbie knew that. "I love you," she said with tears of joy building in her eyes.

"I love you too, Mommy."

Mary stood straight and wiped away the wetness that had formed. "That over there is another room, which will probably be the living room, at least for now." She directed their attention to a doorway, with no actual door, toward the back left side of the kitchen. "As for the rest of the house, it's through the door there." She leaned back and pointed to that massive oak door. "That is another living room. Oh, my, I almost forgot. How could I possibly have forgotten this part," she exclaimed with excitement and frustration as she began walking toward that door.

She paused before entering this other room and turned to look at Marie and Robbie, with Matthew close behind. "This part of the house was built before the Civil War. The rest of the house from here to the living room has been added since then." She walked through the door.

To the left were the wooden steps leading to the second floor. Three of the walls inside had been plastered and drywalled to give a more modern appearance. The fourth wall, though, the one to the right, where Mary was now pointing and showing off, was all stone. In the middle of the sturdy stone wall was a big stone fireplace which had a stone front that protruded a foot or two into the living space, apparently to keep sparks from hitting the wood floors. Above the fireplace was an oak mantle that stretched out five feet. "Isn't this just the most beautifully amazing room you have ever seen!" Before anyone could answer, she walked over to the mantle and pointed at a grayish-black ball and started up again. "OK, so like I said, this part of the house was here before the Civil War. During the Civil War the house was actually fired upon and this cannon ball was later found in the wall where it had hit it!" she proclaimed with an almost boasting attitude.

"That is very interesting and, yes, this is a wonderful house, Mary," Marie responded. "I am so very happy for you and Donnie and your beautiful family." She embraced Mary in an affectionate hug.

"That is cool, Mom, very cool. Did anyone die here during the war?" Robbie questioned, breaking the mood of high emotion. He looked to the floor in shame for asking.

"Honey, I am not sure but think of this... That cannon ball there was found in the wall on the outside of the house, which means not even a cannon could get through the walls. So I would say the people inside, if there were any, were pretty safe. What do you think?" Mary responded with sincerity.

"That's true," he said. Although what he thought was, *Well, that didn't really answer my question, Mom.*

"Well, let's get this cleaning started before the men arrive and wonder what we did all day long," Marie chuckled.

"Yes, Marie, I agree, plus the sooner we start cleaning and putting things in their place, the sooner I will feel at home. Robbie, why don't you go upstairs and look around at the bedrooms? There is also a half bath upstairs, which means it has just a sink and toilet. Then you could go outside and look around as well," Mary replied, happy about the change in subject.

"OK, Mom," Robbie answered, not very excited.

So his mom and grandma, because Marie and Henry said it was OK to call them Grandma and Pappy, took Matt with them back into the kitchen. Robbie turned to look at the steps, not really sure if he wanted to follow them to their destination or just go outside. After a few moments, he decided now would be best time to explore the house because it was the middle of the afternoon and it would be brightest now. He proceeded to the foot of the stairs and looked up first before moving forward. He noticed that while the railing vanished at the point where it intersected the ceiling on this level, there appeared to be no wall upstairs because he could see another railing on the second floor. He put his small hand on the railing and slowly placed his right foot on the bottom step, then jerked it back when the step let out a moan. *Calm down*, he thought to himself, and placed his foot back on the step again. The step made the same sound again, but he heard it for what it really was; the wood creaking beneath his little weight settling. A couple deep breaths and his left foot finally followed, although seemingly unwillingly.

"Stop scaring yourself," he said out loud. But he could not force his body to listen to his demands of movement. Standing there, he realized that all those people he yelled at in the horror movies to run really couldn't—they were trying but they just couldn't. "Well, that's the dumbest thing to think of right now, isn't it?" he said out loud again. He then waited to make sure there was no reply.

Behind him, he could just make out his mother's laughter. She was talking to Marie. This calmed him enough to take the next step up...then the next...and the next, until he proceeded a bit faster, a bit more confident, but just a bit. From the sixth step up he could see light coming from one of the windows that had trapped his mind from just outside the car. Two more steps and the railing was gone. Two more steps and he could see the hallway floor to the right of him through the prongs of the railing that were there to make sure no one could forget where they were and fall down the steps from the side. "Didn't help Damian's mom, though, did it?" he said, and then winced immediately. *No more movies in my head, please*, he begged his brain.

Three more steps up and he was standing on the second floor, looking straight ahead at the wall. He just stood there looking at the wall, because he was fighting with his stupid brain again. "No, it was only twelve steps. I remember, I counted them," he protested aloud. But his debating self said,

"No, you started after you took the first step and thought about understanding why people in those movies don't just run instead of standing there." With a sigh, his shoulders slumped forward, as he realized it was thirteen steps he had just conquered. Then a thought raced through his mind, which was trying to help this time, and he exclaimed with pride, "I was born on the thirteenth, so that number can't be bad all the time, right? Right!"

So he continued exploring. To the right of where he was looking at the wall there was the window, then a couple feet to the right of the window was another wall. As he slowly turned to the right, to see what the upstairs had to offer, he noticed another door, which was shut. It was about fifteen feet down the hallway, on the left side.

He had completed the 180-degree about face, took a side-shift step to his left, and stared down the length of the hallway to another room. This room had another big, solid wood door like the one downstairs, and it was open so he could see into the room. It appeared to be as big as the whole upstairs of their apartment. "Wow, I hope that's my room," he said. He thought of all the space he would have to play, even after the beds and dressers were placed accordingly.

Apparently, he had zero control of his body movements this day because when he finished thinking of how much room he would have to play in, Robbie realized he had walked the breadth of the hallway. Now he was standing just inside the massive bedroom, looking around and smiling. Smiling, of course, until he regained his position in the house and began to think, *Did I actually walk to this spot without knowing it, or did I float here?* "Well, that's dumb, too. Of course I didn't float. I was thinking and walking at the same time and was wrapped up in my thoughts, kind of like Mom says when I sleepwalk sometimes. I just end up places, like the kitchen or her room. I walked here while I was thinking... Same thing as sleeping really," he said out loud.

This bedroom was every bit as big as it looked from the other end of the hallway, probably even bigger. To the left of the doorway was a closet that ran along the twelve-foot wall before it joined the side wall on the left. This wall had nothing to offer, except for one big window, which was placed about halfway down the wall. "That is so cool, I love it!" he exclaimed.

He found himself running to the window. He put his hands on the window ledge and with a small hop he was sitting in the window ledge, looking over the front yard, the big, old garage at the left corner, and the two newer storage-looking sheds to his right. "This is awesome!"

Robbie was sitting on the window ledge, his butt and back against one side of the framework with his hands on his knees, his feet tapping on the other side of the framework. He then turned his attention to the rest of the room and realized this was the only window in what he really hoped would be his new bedroom. Robbie wanted to check the other room out too, and then head outside to explore the yard and buildings. He slid out of the window, tapped the ledge, and said, "I will see you later." He smiled as visions of sitting there reading, doing homework, or just looking outside, listening to his music filled his head.

As he exited the room and reached hallway again, he realized he had walked right past the bathroom. To his left was a sliding door that resembled a window blind, only bigger, of course. This was closed, so Robbie reached out for the handle and slid the door to the right. In an accordion motion, the door opened. His mom was right, the space was just big enough to use the toilet and then wash your hands, but at least he wouldn't have to go all the way downstairs to pee at night.

There wasn't much to see in that room, so he closed the door and turned to face the other bedroom with the closed door. Robbie walked over to the door, turned the knob, and pushed the door open. This room was smaller than "his" bedroom. To the left was the other window he had noticed while outside, and there was a small closet in the righthand corner. This room was small and cold; very cold, actually. Robbie didn't think much of this room, so he left and pranced back down the stairs. He picked up a playful skip as he approached the kitchen.

Mary and Marie were busy cleaning out cupboards, and the room smelled of ammonia with just a hint of flowers. They turned simultaneously in amazement when Robbie bounded into the kitchen with a Christmas morning smile and glow. "Did you like the bedrooms, sweetie?" Mary asked with a giggle.

"Yes, yes, I did. Did you see that big window in the big bedroom, Mommy? I love that window; it is awesome to sit in and look outside or to read in." His blue eyes sparkled.

Marie looked at Mary with a questioning look, because she herself had not gone through the entire house yet. Mary smiled back, but something was different about this smile, Robbie thought. "Honey, of course I did and I knew you would like it, but that room will be Daddy's and mine's. Yours will be the other room, at least until we get some remodeling done," she said. Instantly, she realized she had ruined his overly good mood. "We are going to turn that room with the fireplace into our bedroom, but it will take some time. So be patient, OK?"

"OK, Mom, I will. But I will help Dad as much as possible so it will be done quicker," he said with another glimpse of his big, toothy smile. "I am kind of hungry. Do we have anything to eat here yet?"

"Well, we were just saying the same thing. Marie and I are going to go to the little store over the hill, to see if they have any lunch meat and chips," Mary stated.

"Cool. Can I go too to look around?" Robbie asked, knowing the answer.

"Yes, you can," Marie answered with a smile.

So the group got into the car and drove about a quarter mile over the hill, and to the left was a little convenience store. When they walked inside, the few patrons that were there stopped to look at who just entered. Mary nodded and smiled at them and moved toward the meat case. "Hello, can I get a pound of Virginia baked ham, please?" she asked with a smile.

"You bet," replied the attendant.

As the young girl behind the counter began to thinly slice the ham, she asked, "So, are you all new to the area or just passing through?"

"Yes, we are new. We just bought the stone house, over the hill there behind the church."

Ever so slightly, the counter girl stopped cutting the ham and took a quick glance back, her eyes wide with amazement. No one noticed, though, because the ladies were looking around at the little store and Robbie had found the penny candy and was counting out a 100 for the dollar he had in his pocket.

Mary grabbed the pack of lunch meat and walked through the store, getting bread, mustard, mayo, pickles, and chips. *Very lovely little store*, she thought as she paid for the food. She bought Robbie's candy too, because she thought he deserved the treat. He loved her for that as well.

***

After they said grace for their lunch, Robbie devoured two sandwiches and a handful of chips. He gulped down his water and headed outside to explore the yard and buildings. His mom caught him right before he went out. "Robbie, Dad said not go in the garage until he was with you, because he doesn't think it's a place you should be exploring alone."

This didn't affect him much because he knew there was more than enough to keep him occupied until Dad got home. "OK, Mom. When will Dad and Pappy be here?"

"In about three hours, sweetheart, so not too much longer," his mother assured him.

He walked out the sliding glass door without feeling the need to respond to her. He stopped and looked around to see where he wanted to go first. His Dad was smart; he knew that's where Robbie would want to go and he made sure to make that the first rule of the house. This caused a chuckle of admiration. Dad sure did know him. He knew a boy's mind like a father would.

Once outside the sliding glass door, Robbie walked toward the storage buildings. This spot was on raised ground. He decided to go around the side and back of the house first, then along the other side to the front yard and end with the two small buildings.

So he turned and walked toward the fence to his right. With great pleasure, he noticed this fence was made of wiring and metal poles, not wood that would also have to be whitewashed. One garage to paint was cool, one whole fence row to paint was OK, but to have to paint the length of fence around this whole yard, well, that was just about enough to make someone *sick*. The woods beyond the fence line looked like a great place to explore on another day, so he simply walked along the fence line. The backyard was even bigger than the front, but a lot of the yard was apparently accounted for with a garden almost the size of the house. The ground there was tilled up but had grass and weeds growing in it, since a crop had not been planted this year. Robbie continued along the fence, past the garden area and to the back corner of the yard. Here was a patch of wild flowers. Bright colors illustrated the blossoms on top of bright green stems. *The shade of the trees along the fence must keep the sun off of them for them to stay so pretty,* he thought. He then turned right and followed this line to the corner, where the wire fence met the wood fence.

There in front of him was the one-room schoolhouse his mother said to stay out of. The small brick building looked like it hadn't been cared for in years. All the windows were gone, and the woods beside it seemed to be trying to figure out a way to completely devour it. Robbie noticed more vines growing along the side than before, and the weeds and grass had grown up past the concrete base. They licked at the brick a good three feet off the ground. Robbie took one last look at the structure then moved along the wood fence toward the garage.

After walking the distance between the corners of the yard and arriving at the garage, he could see that this was in need of far more than just a paint job. The garage was basically going to need a complete overhaul, as his dad would say. Robbie then continued his journey around the yard by moving forward, along another wire fence that ran along the front yard perimeter. This fence was by far taller than the rest of the fence lines. Robbie stopped and looked at the barn on the other side of the fence and the rocky terrain. He then turned to his own yard and was glad that all he saw was heavy grass. There was a small hill toward the end of the front yard with a huge oak tree. Robbie thought to himself, *That tree must be very old, over a 100-years-old, easily.*

As he approached the hill, he could see that one of the two smaller buildings appeared to be a chicken coop. A very high and tight mesh fence enclosed an area of about ten square feet. The little building was obviously where the chickens were housed at one time. Robbie thought that was cool and hoped his dad would decide to get some chickens and reopen the coop.

To the right of the coop was the sidewalk that extended alongside the house, then passed the house out to the gate? Robbie wasn't sure. He walked along the concrete then turned left to see the doorway of the second storage building. He turned the handle and pushed to see just what he thought he would see, nothing. Just a storage shed where his dad's shelves would be placed to store his tools and smaller equipment. So he closed the door and looked behind him at the house. Through the window, he could see his mom and grandma were still in the kitchen.

Robbie went back inside and asked if there was anything he could do to help.

***

After his mom gave him a bucket with some Pine-Sol in it and a sponge, Robbie went to the bathroom connected to the kitchen. He worked until he heard the front door open.

It was Dad and Henry! He wiped his hands on his T-shirt and went running through the kitchen and into the dining room, where Mommy was still hugging his new dad (well, his first real one, anyway). So he hugged them both and squeezed real tight.

"Come on, boy, let's go out and get the things from the truck," Donnie said with a smile. "So what do you think of the house?"

"It's very nice. I was a little scared at first but not anymore. I walked all over the yard and went upstairs and was helping Mom till now," the little boy replied excitedly.

"Sounds like a full day for you," Donnie said, not mentioning the being scared part.

"Yes it was!" he exclaimed with joy.

After the truck was unloaded, and the cleaning in the kitchen and bathroom was complete, they all went out for pizza. At dinner, they talked about the plans for the house. Robbie got excited when they discussed changing some rooms around. Eventually, Robbie and Matt would share the big room upstairs.

Robbie fell asleep on the ride back to the house. The excitement of the day and a full belly meant sleep for a young man like him. "Robbie, wake up, wake up, honey," his mother said as she lightly shook him.

As he awoke, he realized he missed the drive home, ah, yes, his new home. But his dad was looking at him and didn't appear to be as happy as he was at dinner. His eyes and face showed a touch of frustration.

"Robbie, I'm not mad, I know you were excited about exploring the house, but you cannot leave the lights on in the house. That costs a lot of money to run lights all day, buddy," Donnie started.

"I know, Daddy, I wouldn't do that," he answered honestly.

"Well then, why is the light on upstairs in your bedroom? Your mom said you were the only one to go upstairs today, and you told me that too," Donnie reminded him.

"I didn't turn the lights on, I swear, Daddy. It was bright today when I went up there. I didn't need the lights. I didn't really even go in that room. I just peeked in and left. I promise," Robbie responded. He was more awake now and more defensive.

His mother always reminded him to keep the lights off whenever he left a room, because she didn't have the money to light rooms just for the carpet to see the roof. So he *always* made sure he turned the lights out. Furthermore, he was sure he never turned those on.

His dad looked at him in a questioning manner and said, "Well, you and I are going to go upstairs and turn it off, OK?"

"OK, Daddy," Robbie answered. He held Donnie's gaze. There was no need to drop his head in shame. He didn't turn the light on.

***

So they all went inside, and his dad led him up the stairs. They went across the hallway to the closed door of the smaller room. *Closed door? Did I close the door when I left today?* Robbie thought. *I don't remember closing the door. I just turned and went down the stairs, didn't I? OK, stop it. Stop it! Enough!*

But he couldn't help it and his mind began to race faster and faster. *Who closed the door? Who turned the light on? Oh, my, this isn't good!*

Donnie opened the door all the way and Robbie felt that cold air again. His dad walked in, turned, and said, "Now, Robbie, I believe you didn't *mean* to leave the light on and I know you were excited, but you have to be sure you turn the lights off. You hear me?" This was the sternest he'd ever heard his father.

"Daddy, I didn't. I know I didn't leave the light on. Mommy doesn't like me leaving lights on either. I always make sure I turn them off," he stated in his own firm, defensive manner.

"Well then, I guess the light turned itself on then, huh?" Donnie said sarcastically.

"Well, yes, I guess." Robbie didn't like the answer he gave, but he couldn't think of anything better.

"Well, lights don't just turn themselves on and off," Donnie said a bit sharper. "We are done here. Just make sure you remember to turn the lights off from now on."

Donnie stepped toward Robbie, who had not actually stepped into the room. He reached for the light switch and flipped it off. Robbie stepped back to keep space between them, and Donnie shut the door and walked straight to the stairs, with Robbie in tow.

***

After Marie and Henry left, the family laid out a couple sleeping bags, comforters, and pillows for a sleepover in their new home. All the furniture was packed neatly into the moving van parked in the driveway. The official grand opening of the house would be tomorrow.

Robbie lay down next to his mom said goodnight to the dark. His mother and father both said goodnight and told him they loved him. With a smile, he quickly drifted off to sleep.

***

Robbie finished playing in the big bedroom; another intense battle between G.I. Joe forces and their arch nemesis, the Cobra. He headed out toward the hallway and the light shut off behind him. He stopped, looked back, confused, and flipped the light switch back on. He turned and began his walk down the hallway again. Suddenly, the hallway became dark again. "What is going on?" he questioned, and proceeded back to the room.

He reached around the corner again and turned the light on. This time, he stood there for a minute to make sure it stayed on. But as soon as he walked away, the light went off yet again. Robbie was getting mad now. He snapped around, reached over, and...SMACK!

His hand was slapped away from the light switch! Robbie recoiled and took a few stumbling steps back, away from the room. His jaw was unhinged and hanging wide open in a startled, dumbfounded expression, like watching a movie where the lead character is killed. His eyes were as wide as they could open without popping out of their sockets. His body developed a shiver that was uncontrollable. *RUN RUN RUN RUN*, he thought. But, like before, his mind and body weren't on the same page. Heck, they were reading two different books!

Then suddenly there was a flash from where the switch is. *RUN RUN RUN*, but there was still no response from his legs.

Slowly, a shape came into view from just inside the room. Was it a ball of some kind? Slowly, ever so slowly, the shape was moving toward him. *OH, GOD, JUST RUN ALREADY!*

Now the shape was visible for what it truly was. There before him was a hand clenching into a tight fist. The hand slowly relaxed and the index finger rose as the wrist portion of the hand rotated up. Robbie's heart was pounding in his chest and he couldn't get a grip on what he was seeing. *A hand doesn't just float by itself, and it had touched me,* he thought. Then the hand rotated 180 degrees and began to make a beckoning motion with the extended, ghostly finger.

"Come... Come... Come... Play with me for a while," a voice from inside the room offered.

To Robbie's surprise, his feet moved forward a step and the hand reciprocated by gliding back ever so slightly. "Yes, that's a good boy. I want to play and I know you will like it." The voice smiled and can't be seen, only heard.

Robbie took another step toward the room. Why? Why was his body refusing to listen to his mind's urgent request to run? This voice and that awful hand were controlling his movement at will. The hand moved back toward the room and the darkness; the extended finger still requested his presence.

Robbie began to take another step and his mind forced his vocal cords into action. "Stop!" His foot fell in line beside the other, without gaining or losing ground on the room. The hand started to retreat farther into the darkness but stopped as well and, for a second, stopped the insistent request.

"You don't want to stop, you want to start. Start playing all the fun games I have for you in the darkness," the voice assured Robbie.

This time, however, Robbie took a step away from the dark, away from the hand. "No, I don't. I am scared and I want to go downstairs," Robbie pleaded. He was slightly stuttering in fear.

"Nothing to fear in here. I just want to play. What kid doesn't enjoy playing games?" the hand rebutted.

Another step backward, and another. He moved slowly, keeping that terrible hand in his view. "No, I don't want to play now, thank you, though. Maybe later, OK?"

"No, I want to play *now!*" The voice was forceful and angrily demanding now. The darkness from the room seemed to grow even darker. The hand rotated downward and back around so the finger pointed at Robbie "And I want to play with you!" All the fingers on the hand sprang forward. It shot out like jack being released from his box.

Robbie ran down the stairs like a sprinter. He didn't even realize how fast he was moving, but he still feels a slight brush of the hand on the back of his shirt as he dropped down the first couple steps. He bounded down the stairs in just a few steps and slammed into the wall when he reached the bottom. He fell to the floor, hard and fast. He could feel the hand grabbing at his clothes, trying to secure him in its clutch. "NOOOO!" Robbie screamed in protest.

"Robbie, Robbie," the voice said. Wait, that voice was different. "Robbie, wake up!"

***

Robbie's eyes exploded open. He was now fighting off the hands of his mother. "Sweetie, please, calm down... Calm down," she pleads with her son. "It was just a dream, baby, just a dream."

Robbie looked toward the stairs, and once his rapid breathing slowed, he began to cry.

***

Robbie awoke in the morning, after a second attempt of sleep, which resulted in no dream at all, thankfully. It was partly due to the commotion of the move. He exited the room without a single glance at the stairs. His dad noticed him first and said, "Good morning, buddy. I hope you slept better after that dream."

Mary turned to look at Robbie as he responded. "Yeah, I did. Sorry I woke everyone up."

She hugged her little man. "It's OK, baby. That must have been a wild dream. I have never seen you so upset before. Your body was crawling with goose bumps and shaking all over." She kissed him on both cheeks.

"I don't really want to talk about it, if that's OK," Robbie begged.

"Of course, that's fine. Let's enjoy the beautiful day and get our house set up," she said with a smile.

***

Over the next couple weeks, the family continued to put everything in place and turn their house into a warm, loving home. Robbie's anxiety over the house did not decrease, though. He spent as little time as he could upstairs. He stayed close to his parents or outside exploring and riding his bike. Bedtime presented serious problems for the boy. Not only did he need to go upstairs, but he had to be there, in the dark, where the shadows and sounds of the house seemed to come alive. He kept his eyes closed, with the blankets pulled safely up to his eyes. The blankets, however, didn't suppress the dream... Oh, that dream. The same one, over and over, repeating like a record skipping on its turntable. Continuing to haunt him, torture him... The night became his enemy, his room became his dungeon.

Robbie was not the only family member experiencing strange and unexplainable events. Though Mary kept these moments to herself. She was not consumed by the feeling of dread and fear as her son was, but she was still very scared at what was transpiring. Robbie's sleepwalking had started again too.

On the third night of their stay in her dream home, Mary was startled awake by a noise...a muffled voice...mumbling. Mary turned in her bed, toward the sounds, and stared into a shadow looking over her and mumbling in a fast, incomprehensible speech. She let out a scream that woke Donnie, who jumped out of bed to find Robbie standing beside the bed, looking at his mother. Mary now realized who owned the shadow.

She slowly sat up as Robbie's babble continued. Unsure of how to proceed, she slowly and quietly said, "Robbie, sweetie, let's go back to bed."

Unfazed by the voice of his mother, Robbie continued. As she touched his shoulder, Robbie stopped so abruptly that Mary yanked her hand back as if to avoid being bitten by an animal. Robbie had been staring at his mother's pillow, but now he turned his head slowly toward his mother. With closed eyes, he said in a low, unknown voice, "I want to play and I want to play with you." A smile spread across his face. It was a smile that didn't seem to fit her little boy. Chills consumed Mary and Donnie. Mary had witnessed her son sleepwalk before, but this was different. This was horrifying.

Suddenly Robbie fell to the ground like a puppet whose strings had been severed. Mary quickly reached the floor to comfort her son. However, Robbie was still asleep and that smile was gone. Donnie carefully picked him up and carried him off to bed, where he placed his son and tucked him back in.

***

A couple nights later, Mary was roused from her sleep to the sound of sweet, soft music. She smiled as she stirred, because the music was so soothing and peaceful. As she opened her eyes the music continued, and the source of the music revealed itself. There before her eyes, about a foot above her head, danced five tiny instruments. A harp, a violin, a trumpet, a saxophone, and a clarinet. An unfamiliar light illuminated the little band, which played a comforting symphonic tune. Although Mary knew she was awake, she passed this off as a layover of her dreams and closed her eyes and drifted off to sleep. In the morning, she wrote the entire event off as a sweet dream. *I mean, seriously, instruments don't dance in the air, playing a song all by themselves,* she told herself in a reassuring voice.

There were also countless cupboard doors that wouldn't keep closed, regardless of who closed them. Clothes seemed to unfold themselves from time to time, if given enough alone time on the bed or washroom counter. It didn't take much time for Donnie and Mary to realize there was something different with the house, and neither one of them seemed to mind saying it was a ghost or spirit.

The happenings in the house were very minor and amusing to some degree. That is, of course, to everyone but Robbie. He was still having that dreadfully awful dream. He still heard the murmur of the house and the steps of unwelcomed guests as everyone else slept. The stress this created was immense and only intensified when he tried to explain to his parents what was happening. They would tell him what every kid hates to hear, whether it was true or not—as in this particular case. "Robbie, you are making yourself scared with your own imagination" and "You really need to stop watching those scary movies."

However, other than the nightmare and the unexplained sounds, there weren't any substantial frightening experiences. That was, until a few months later.

***

Robbie's parents had gone out for their anniversary and left the three kids (by this point, Mary had given birth to the newest family member six weeks ago; Leslie was her first little girl) at home with a few family members. Robbie loved his cousins and his uncle very much. He always enjoyed when they were around. It was a great day of fun and games and movies and laughter. But as we all know, all good things must come to an end, and this was Robbie's first true lesson in this rule.

"Alright, big boy, it's time for you to go to bed," his Uncle Barry announced.

Robbie looked at his uncle and asked to stay up just a while longer. When his uncle said no, Robbie walked up to him and asked, "Can I talk to you in the kitchen please?"

Barry chuckled and said, "Sure, dude. Let's go."

"OK, look... I am really scared of this house, Uncle Barry, and I don't want to go upstairs. Can I please stay down here and sleep with you all?"

Barry smiled and said, "Come on, buddy. I'll go up with you and check things out so you can sleep in peace."

He reached down and grabbed Robbie's hand and led him to the stairs to the room. Barry turned the lights on and checked each closet to ensure there were no monsters waiting for him to leave. However, not all monsters can be seen.

Robbie crawled into his bed and got under his protective covers, preparing for his defensive strategy, unaware of how bad tonight was going to be. "Now I lay me down to sleep, I pray the Lord my soul to keep, if I die before I wake, I pray the Lord my soul to take," he prayed softly.

Uncle Barry walked to the door, turned to Robbie, smiled, and said, "See ya in the morning, buddy. Love ya."

"Love you too," Robbie weakly replied.

Barry turned the light off and closed the door. Robbie heard his footfalls weaken as he walked away, down the hallway and down the stairs, across the house to the living room where everyone was anxiously waiting to hear what was going on.

Robbie closed his eyes and wished he would fall asleep, which was actually the best way to stay awake, but he didn't know that, of course. In no time, Robbie heard those ghastly steps approaching his door and he felt cold air suddenly surround him. As Robbie hid his eyes under the comforter, he heard the knob turning slow, which sent a slight metal on metal screech in his direction. Then the hinges began to whine as the door is opened slightly, then a bit more. Then there was nothing, no sound, no movement, other than the familiar underside of his shield. Through nerves, curiosity, and a sense of bravery he didn't know he had, Robbie slowly, slowly, slowly pulled the cover from his head, stopping just below his vision. He still couldn't see the door. Was it really that dark inside his room? The moon usually lit up the room slightly.

As these thoughts, among others, raced through his head, he remembered he was pulling down the cover so he could see. He knew he needed to open his eyes to see what was happening at his door. He raised his hand to his eyes so he could open them with a sense of protection before facing whatever might be waiting for him. Fear is a normal feeling that we all experience at multiple times in our life, but this level of fear to a child was bordering on mind breaking.

Robbie opened his eyes, instantly removing his hand from his face, fearing that the hand from his dream had come to life to finish what it had tried to do so often in his sweating terrors of rest. Just as his eyes adjusted to the moonlit room and focused on the doorway, the door slammed shut with such a force that the rush of air that swept over his bed caused his sheet to waver. Before Robbie had time to react, the door opened again but this time with quicker intent. Then repeatedly, the door opened and shut, over and over again. The force was hard enough to splinter the door frame. A deep and deliberate chuckle started that caused the blood in Robbie's body to freeze instantly.

"I want to play," the darkness insisted.

"Mommy, please help me, Mommy," Robbie prayed to himself over and over and over again.

"No help needed, sonny. Just come play with me. You will love the games we will play," the voice implored.

Starting to cry, Robbie pleaded with the voice, "Please, leave me alone. I just want to sleep. I don't want to play games with anyone. I am scared and just want to sleep now."

"If you play with me, you will never be scared again, I promise you that…Robbie." The horrid voice softly but sadistically said his name.

After a few minutes had passed, Robbie thought the nightmare before him had finally stopped. That's when the voice sounded out more assertively and bolder than before. "You can choose to play or I can make you play. It doesn't matter to me, but you will play eventually and there is nothing you can do to stop me...boy!"

Then the door flew open completely and there stood a figure in the doorway. It didn't step into view, it was just there. The figure made no further advances into the room. He simply, slowly raised one arm and extended his index finger to point at the boy and shouted with an ear-deafening explosion, "You will play, boy, you will play, I promise you!!"

Robbie did the only thing he could think of. He grabbed the covers and covered his head and began to scream for his mother to save him. Over and over again, he screamed and screamed to the point his throat began to strain with the tension in his neck.

Then a hand reached out to him and began to shake him. As the covers were removed from his head, Robbie began to fight. He was swinging his arms and striking out at the man who stood over him, threatening to play his games at will.

"Robbie... Robbie, stop! Come on, buddy, wake up. Wake up, buddy," the voice said now. Only this voice sounded familiar. Yes! This voice he knew!

Robbie opened his eyes and there stood his uncle, who looked frightened and confused too.

"Did you see him too, Uncle Barry? Did you see the man by my door? Does he want to play with you too?" Robbie cried to him.

"What man, buddy? There's no man here but me. You had a bad dream, buddy, but you are alright now. I'm here and it's alright," his uncle said, trying to console him.

Robbie looked his uncle in the eye, controlled his breathing, and lightly whispered, "He was there. No dream, not this time, and he wants to play a game, but I won't play and he is very mad at me."

With that, Robbie passed out, and slept a long peaceful sleep without dreams for the first time in a long time.

***

When he woke up the next day, his mother was sitting on the floor by his bed, with a look of fear and love in her eyes. She slowly reached out to him, caressed his face, and said, "Good morning, angel. I heard you had a bad night."

Robbie began to cry and went to his mother, who rocked him and sang softly to him. The comfort of a mother's arms seemed to always ward off the demons. This particular one would take more than that, though.

Robbie relived the entire night to his mom and dad. He corrected them each time they insisted he had been dreaming. Robbie pleaded with them to take him out of that room. He told them he never wanted to sleep there again. All he asked was to stay up with them and sleep in bed with them forever. So after Mary ensured Donnie this was the only solution she would accept for the time being, that is what happened.

***

Although the cupboards still opened at will and the clothes never seemed to be folded right, Robbie's nightmares and visions stopped. He slept peacefully and without fear. However, Donnie wasn't too excited about him sleeping between them each and every night. He wouldn't be able to stand it for much longer. So after a long conversation with Mary, it was decided that they would buy Robbie the dog of his choice to help him feel protected all the time, but especially while he slept.

Robbie was excited about this. He had never had a pet before, and to have a dog that could fight off the bad man, well, that was just awesome!

A NEW FRIEND

So Donnie and Robbie left the house to start the search. Donnie had heard of a small country store in West Virginia that was selling Chow Chows. Donnie had told Robbie about Chows and he was beaming with anticipation as they left the house. When they reached the store and walked inside, Donnie asked the clerk if they still had dogs for sale. The clerk mindlessly pointed to the back of the store and said what was left was in a pen. They couldn't miss them.

Robbie was already pulling his dad toward the treasure in the back. When they reached the wooden pen, Robbie looked over and saw the cutest puppies he had ever seen, which wasn't many, but he just knew they were the cutest. As his dad got down on a knee and started to ask his son which one he wanted, all the puppies rushed to the side of the pen. All accept one. This puppy stood stoically in the back and was twice the size of the others. It slowly and confidently walked through the gaggle of yipping pups, looked into Robbie's eyes, and Robbie looked into his and the bond was set in stone. In Robbie's mind, he heard, *I will protect you from the bad man. That's why you found me so easily.* The boy blinked and shook his head, because the words were real. They weren't his thoughts but the thoughts of the animal before him. And how did he know about the bad man?

"That one, Daddy, the big one right there!" he exclaimed, pointing and almost leaping through the ceiling.

"Well... Now, Robbie, that one looks like he is older than the rest. Let me check with the girl first, OK?" His dad walked up front to where the clerk was.

Robbie looked back at the dog and he was still standing there looking up him while the other puppies jumped and barked for attention. Robbie thought to the big dog, *Did you talk to me in my head?*

Without any delay, the dog barked a solid and short bark. Not a puppy yip, either, but a true, mature bark that shocked the boy and caused a moment of doubt, which was wiped away quickly when he heard, *We were meant to find each other.*

Donnie returned to the pen, smiling, and informed his ecstatic boy that the puppy was not older, just bigger, and came with papers. *Whatever that means*, Robbie thought.

Robbie reached down and said ecstatically, "Come here, boy, you are going home with me!"

Once they got back to the house, Robbie couldn't wait to show everyone his new best friend, Bandit. That's what his dad and he had come to agree on in the car, and Bandit didn't seem to mind the name either.

Mary fell in love with Bandit right away. She loved how his tail curled up on his back, and his cute purplish-black tongue was the icing on the cake. No one could get over how big he was, and Donnie commented that because of the size of his head and paws, Bandit was sure to be a beast of a dog.

***

That night, Robbie was willing to try to sleep in his room, with Bandit in the bed with him. He fell asleep while petting Bandit. Carefully, he stroked his fur from the back of his neck to the top of his head, because his dad had said this was how you pet a Chow.

While Robbie slept peacefully, Bandit was stirred awake by a feeling of hate and coldness. As he opened his young eyes, his mature mind picked up on the feeling of something else in the room, and it was a something he didn't like. Bandit slowly rose up in bed and looked around the room. He couldn't see anything, but that feeling was growing hotter in his senses as the air he sucked in grew colder still. Then a breeze blew against him and Bandit began to pick up on a shape across the room. Bandit's eyes locked in on the shape as he stepped over the young boy and stood at the side of the bed. He dropped his head slightly, pulled back his lips, and bared his very sharp puppy teeth and let out a low but sustained growl—one you would never expect to come from such a young dog. Bandit had drawn his line in the sand with the figure before him and had no plans of backing down.

The shape stood still for a moment then the head tilted back and a light laugh emerged. It looked back at Bandit and said, "You're the hero? You have been chosen to stop me? That little boy is mine, and you can do nothing to stop me."

However, the shape made no attempt to move toward the bed, and Bandit was still peering at him, growling his intentions.

Fear is something every dog can sense, and Bandit sensed it right now. What he was trying to work out was whether the fear he sensed was the figure's or if it was the fear of others emanating *from* the figure. But that wasn't important now.

What mattered was Robbie. Nothing was going to happen to him without Bandit giving it his all to defend him.

"Get down and move away from him, young soldier," the figure requested. But Bandit only growled stronger and louder.

The shape took a step into the light and Bandit could now see his face. It caused alarm in his young soul, yet he stood his ground. The face was long and shallow. The eyes were slightly bigger than those he had seen and seemed to glow. Not a white light, but the blue in his eyes illuminated the room. The old clothes hanging off him were dirty and full of holes. He smelled of death.

Bandit dropped his head very low and crouched down in a position of attack. He pulled his lips back to the point where the muscles in his face tightened. He then opened his mouth to show all the pain that could be inflicted by his powerful jaws. He deepened his growl, making a demonic sound. Bandit kept his keen eyes locked on his target, locked on the true essence of the thing standing before him. The fear he sensed intensified, and Bandit was confident he was going to win this standoff.

The shape stared back into the dog's eyes and realized this wouldn't be easy. This infuriated him. He had waited for the boy's parents to make him sleep in his own room, alone for easy pickings. Now a new guardian had been introduced, and this one was going to be very bothersome. "You and I will have to play first, mutt," the shaped informed Bandit. This time it his tone wasn't confident or controlling. It knew it had been defeated, this time. The man at the door faked a smile, and then faded into the darkness of the room.

Bandit maintained his vigilant stance a while longer, then slowly relaxed his face, stood upright, and cut off the growl that had seemed to keep bellowing from the depths of his gut. His throat was raw, his muscles were tight and sore, but his pride was overflowing. He had stood his ground against an evil thing he couldn't quite comprehend and he had bested him. He had beaten it this time and he knew there would be more times to come, but Bandit also knew that each time he faced the man, Bandit would be older, bigger, stronger, and more aware of his own powers.

And still Robbie slept without dreaming.

***

For several months, the boy and his dog...his friend...his companion, played outside, went for walks through the woods, and built a bond that was stronger than any he had ever felt (well, next to his mother, of course). Robbie loved Bandit and it was easy to see to that Bandit loved him right back. The two were never apart when Robbie was home. When he came home from school, Bandit would be waiting for Robbie by the front gate and would jump up at him in excitement. Best friends. Yeah, they were definitely best friends.

As this time passed, Bandit grew large and muscular. He was by far the biggest Chow Donnie had ever seen or heard of, and while he was extremely protective of the kids and the home, he could also be sensitive and loving, especially with Robbie.

Robbie's horrors didn't end during this time, but he didn't have as many terrifying experiences either. He had his dream from time to time, but Bandit always seemed to wake him up before the dream escalated. The door to his room would open and close at night and slam shut from time to

The Game Evil Plays

time, but once Bandit growled or barked, the door stayed shut. Robbie didn't cry anymore when the scary stuff started and to some degree, it had become a game to him. The man wanted to play games after all and Robbie was starting to like this game—as long as Bandit was there, of course.

HISTORY – THE STEVENSON GAMES

MARY COULDN'T BELIEVE what she was reading. How could these things have happened for so long, and who could commit such horrors? And in her beautiful house? Those poor families. Those poor, poor people.

***

In August of 1862, Dale Plush, a vagabond, became the school teacher in a small starter town called Stevenson. Slain bodies had been found within his home when Southern soldiers used it as a base camp, leading up to the Battle of Antietam. The soldiers arrived on his property in the middle of the night, and as they searched the house, Dale was found in bed, sleeping with two corpses, his latest victims. Shocked and horrified, the commander of the brigade had Dale removed from the house, questioned him, and then hung him from a tree on the property. The bodies were buried in the field adjacent to the house.

While being questioned, Dale recounted how he had played a game with everyone from the small town over the hill. He had manipulated them with lies and then killed them all. Afterwards, he burnt the whole town down with the flames of hell. He continued to elaborate on his games and claimed he did the work of the devil. And then he smiled...

Dale walked down the dirt road, searching for the perfect place to begin his next series of games. All he carried was a backpack with some clothes, an extra pair of shoes, and his teaching books. Besides the pleasure he received from torturing and killing his contestants, teaching was something he really enjoyed. He had always wanted to be a teacher, but the killing had kept him on the move. The torture was new, though. It was his new game and he enjoyed playing it so much.

Dale had been walking for a few weeks, stopping at a few towns along the way, until he came upon the perfect setup. There before him was a stone house, off the side of the road, in a field with wooded areas on two sides of it. On the third side was a small structure, which could easily be fixed and used to teach. Dale walked knocked twice on the front door, but there was no answer. He walked around the house and there was a garden in the backyard. There he saw two people hunched over, working the rows of food. Dale walked up to the edge of the garden and said, "Excuse me, ma'am, is the man of the house home?"

Startled, the woman and her daughter looked up and squinted against the sunshine. "I'm sorry, but my husband isn't home, he's down the road working the farm. May I help you?"

"Well, ma'am, my name is Dale Plush, and I was wondering if I might be able to stay here a couple nights to rest up? I could stay over there in that building if it suits you better," Dale said with a friendly smile.

The woman stood, rubbed her hands on her apron, looked over to the storage shed, and said, "My name is Elizabeth Wolf, this here is Rebecca, and my husband's name is John. I don't know if that will be a comfortable rest for you, sir, but I see no trouble in that. When John comes home I will have him come see you, so you can talk to him about your intentions. Would you like some water? You look dried out."

"Thank ya, ma'am, I would love some water. I also wouldn't mind giving you a hand with your chores as payment for your hospitality." He wore a devilish smile, knowing how this would end.

"Well, the pump is around front there. You can fill your cup as much as you need and if you're still inclined to help, come see me. We got us enough to keep the three of us busy till the second coming," Elizabeth said with a friendly smile and chuckle. She would see her Lord soon enough, though.

Dale got his water and washed some through his hair and over his face. He drank another cup and thought this place was just right. He then walked over to the building he considered his schoolhouse and opened the big doors. Straw and hay covered the floor and there were bales along the side walls. Other than that there was nothing else. He dropped his bag, stretched, and began to devise a plan.

***

"What would you like me to start with, ma'am?" Dale asked as he returned to the woman and her beautiful little girl.

"Well, we need more wood chopped if your back is up to it. Becca, please show Mr. Plush where the ax and chopping block are. John has some wood set up there already," Elizabeth answered.

"Yes, Mama. Follow me, Mr. Plush," Becca said enthusiastically.

Becca walked Dale over to the side of the house, by one side of the woods, and said, "Daddy likes us to cut up the wood here, then carry it over there, and stack it up neatly for when we need it."

"Thank ya, Becca. I will try to do your daddy proud," Dale said slyly.

Becca smiled and giggled, then walked back to her mother to finish her work in the garden. Dale picked up the ax, enjoying the feeling of the hard wood handle and the weight of the metal head. That smile crept across his face again as he set up the first piece of wood. He steadied the head of the weapon over the defenseless wood, slowly rotated his shoulders, and drove his arms downward emphatically, splitting the wood with ease in one single, fluid movement. My, how he loved that feeling. He thought of all the memories, as his member began to swell. He chopped another piece of wood, then another, and another. He was no longer splitting wood in his mind. His visions were much, much worse than that.

After hours of working, only stopping to quench his thirst and stretch, the pile of wood was split. All he needed to do now was carry the pile to the overhang, which kept the split wood dry. As he finished stacking the wood, Becca came over to check on his progress.

"Mama wants to know if you're hungry, Mr. Plush."

"Well, I sure could use some good cookin', if your mama doesn't mind," Dale responded.

"I will let her know. *Wow*, I can't believe you got all this done already. Daddy is gonna like you," Becca said cheerfully.

Unfortunately, Daddy *would* like Mr. Plush...but he'd have to live long enough.

***

After lunch was served and the table was cleaned, Dale said he was in need of some rest. The long days of walking, the work, and the good food were all weighing on him. So he excused himself to the barn but asked to be called on once John had returned home so he could talk with him.

John returned home shortly after sunset, as was normal for the farmer. Sweaty, dirty, and exhausted, he walked through the front door and was met, as usual, by his loving daughter and wife. He was quickly informed that they had a guest sleeping in the barn and that Mr. Dale Plush wanted John to wake him up so they could talk about a short stay.

John walked to the barn and opened the door. The stranger lay on the floor, and John saw a book beside him through the glow of his lantern. As John walked closer he also saw a knife. John had a knife just like that, which he used to skin and clean the wildlife he killed.

Dale woke with a start and reached for the knife. John exclaimed, "Hang on there, stranger, I'm John... This is my home and you are my guest. Grabbing a knife to use on me isn't proper." John smiled.

Dale placed the knife back on the ground and stood. He was a bit taller than six feet and was lean and muscular. However, he still had to look up to John, who stood about three to four inches taller, with broad, heavy shoulders and big arms. However, no fear entered Dale, just caution.

"I apologize, sir. Being on the road for as long as I have teaches a man to be ready for ambushes from those looking to pick on a solitary Christian. My name is Dale Plush, and it is my pleasure to meet you." Dale extended his right hand.

John returned the gesture and the two men shook. "Well, that is understandable, apology accepted. My name is John, John Wolf. Welcome to my home. Why don't you get yourself together and come inside for dinner, and then we can talk."

Dale said that sounded good to him. John smiled and nodded then turned and walked to the house. For a minute, Dale just stared at John as his lantern light faded into the darkness. Dale put his shirt and boots on then headed into the house.

With dinner warming their bodies, the two men stepped outside on the porch and sat down to talk. John asked Dale the normal questions: Where are you from? Where are you going? Do you have any family?

Dale was guarded with his responses, but had prepared well for the easy inquiries. Dale worked through these questions then started on some of his own. "Are you all from here?"

"Actually, we are not. We're from North Carolina. That's where our families live. We came up this way ten years ago. I worked for a man who drove cattle and horses to this part of the country. I fell in love with this land. That was just after Beth and I married. When I got back home, I told her of my intentions to move here. If she wanted to stay in Carolina, I understood, but she's a good woman and she made the trip with me. We settled here and Becca was born nine months later. The folks around here are simple and solitary. It's quiet. Good place to raise a family away from the war," John explained.

John was wrong about that, though. He just didn't know it yet.

After talking some more, John leaned over and said, "Beth tells me you wish to stay with us for a time. She also tells me that you work hard and seem to be genuine in your intentions. How long were you thinking about staying? And if you don't mind me asking so bluntly, what are your intentions, exactly?"

Dale had thought this through. "Well, John, I would have to say I'm not completely sure. Maybe my time here would depend on if you could tell me how close I am to the next town. I am looking for a place to start my teaching up again. I do miss teaching the youth the ways of the world and educating them so they can become whatever it is they set out to be."

John leaned back, chuckled, and said, "Dale, your travels may indeed be over. Just over the hill there, about twenty minutes with a buggy, is Stevenson. It's not a big, thriving town, but a community nonetheless. Around this area you may be the only true teacher. Most folks educate their kids themselves."

Dale could not believe his luck, and the surprise showed on his face. All the pieces were falling into place. He was truly blessed.

"That sounds just perfect. I may walk into town tomorrow and see if I can find some folks to talk to about setting up here. I also need to find a place where my lessons could be taught. Oh, and I'll probably need to clean up a bit," he said. He looked at his clothes, took a deep sniff, coughed, and started to laugh.

John laughed too, and the two men finished their coffee, discussed the war, politics, and religion... A typical conversation between men. While they talked and bonded, Dale's mind raced on how he was going to relieve Mr. Wolf of his property and his life.

***

Dale slept long and peacefully. When he woke up, the heat of the day was already filling the barn. He stretched and dressed and headed to the house for coffee and hopefully a bath. Dale was surprised to see John working in the garden with his family. He walked over toward them and John said, "Well, good morning, Dale. Wasn't sure if you wanted to sleep in or if I should wake ya. I figured you needed some good rest after all your travels. If it isn't too forward, I thought I would stay here today to guide you to town and help you meet up with some town folks. I need some supplies as well, so it would work out for us both." John stood and wiped his hands on his pants leg.

Dale couldn't resist grinning, because he was in a no-lose situation. He hadn't done anything and his plan was already working. This was his chance for the town folk to see John and him together, talking, laughing, and buying supplies—all the things men do when they are working together.

Dale said, "John, I'm not sure how I'll ever repay you for your hospitality. That sounds like a grand idea, but I wonder if I could trouble you for a bath and a place to soak these rags. I cannot bare the smell, and I am sure you all would appreciate the absence of my odor." He laughed.

John led Dale inside. The pots were warming on the wood stove for his pre-planned bath. John also showed him where he could toss his clothes for his wife to clean later.

Dale was on cloud nine as he sat in the tub and allowed his body to soak in the warmth of the water. He washed away the dirt and smell of constant travel. As he dressed in his clean clothes, he felt recharged and ready for the events to come... Those to come soon and those that still needed more time to hatch.

John had the wagon hooked up to the horses and was set to go. He waved to Dale as he exited the house and Dale couldn't help himself, so he waved back and smiled. *What a day, what luck, what a life!*

***

The ride into town wasn't long. The men had just enough time to discuss what supplies they needed. The first stop was the feed shop, where Dale helped John carry feed sacks and seeds to the wagon.

Everyone seemed to really like John and they were welcoming toward Dale. Dale put on his best smiles and how-do-ya do's, which everyone just ate up. Then they headed over to the clothing store, where Dale was surprised when John told him to get himself a couple pairs of pants and some shirts. John told Dale he could work off the cost of the clothes at the house or the farm. John walked to the women's side and picked up some fabric that Beth had asked for, along with some sewing items. The clerk in the store, Bill, asked John about the family and how the farm was doing. John let him know everyone was doing great and the farm was doing well too. John then introduced Dale, saying he was new to town and was staying with them for the time being. "He is looking to get a school up and running but until he can do that, he will be working at the house and the farm for room and board."

Bill extended his hand and greeted Dale, "Welcome to Stevenson. A school, huh? Well, you will want to talk to James West. He is the so-called mayor of our little town. With John here on your side you probably won't have much trouble with him, seeing how James is infatuated with Beth." He laughed.

They left the store, loaded their packages into the wagon, and walked to the Town Hall building, where James was at his desk, looking over the town's income. *Bill sure knew what he was talking about,* Dale thought, because James started the conversation with, "Well, John, hello there. How is that beautiful wife of yours doing these days?"

The two talked for a minute and seemed pleasant toward each other, then John changed the topic.

"James, this here is Dale Plush. He is new to the area and staying with us for the time being. He would like to talk to you about doing some teaching around here."

James stood with a shocked expression, but he was already considering the possibility of adding a school to the town. This was something the townsfolk had discussed before, but they couldn't come up with the money.

"Well, welcome to Stevenson, Mr. Plush. Welcome, indeed," James said, smiling.

"Thank you, Mr. West. I hope we aren't catching you at a bad time, but I would like to discuss starting a school, like John stated. Is this something you and your town would be interested in?" Dale inquired.

"Have a seat please, Mr. Plush. Yes, we have talked about starting up a school for our children, but we don't have the funds to get started and there are a small amount of children in this town. This isn't a poor area, sir, but we don't like to tax our folks too much and we don't think the people would pay for something they're already doing themselves, even if it isn't a grade-A education. Most of the kids here will be farmers and cattle ranchers like their fathers. So there's the dilemma, front and center, just so you know," James said.

Dale found this amusing. He had this entire town in his hands. *I must have been a good boy,* he thought. How else could all of his fortunes be explained?

With a smile and deep sincerity, Dale interjected, "James, I believe I may have misled you, sir. I am not asking to be paid for my work. I teach because I feel it is my duty to God to provide an education for the youth. I enjoy teaching. I enjoy the look in a child's eyes when they realize they fully understand what they are being taught. All I need is a place to teach. A room, a building, a church, or even here would be just fine. I just need enough room so the kids can sit and listen to my instruction. I will continue to work for John and his family, to cover my room and board, if that works for him. I am a simple man, with a simple pleasure, and I am not looking for riches. Just knowing that I've helped the young people expand their knowledge of reading and math is good enough for me." This came out so easily and so fluidly that it almost surprised him. He could tell, just by looking at them, that he had won. He just needed to stop talking. He chuckled to himself again; he was the pied piper.

James couldn't believe what he was hearing. This stranger was willing to come into their town and help mold their young people and do it without pay of any sort. He couldn't wait for this man to stop talking so he could say yes. Yes, they would find a place for him to teach.

"I will just need a little time to get ready for the classes. Make up some lesson plans and things of that sort. I would guess that in two weeks I should be able to start the classes. I know it's summer but I also know the children will be needed at harvest time. We can do some classes now and until then. Then we can start back up after the season is over. That way the families won't be missing the extra hands during their peak season. Does this suit you, sir?"

Doesn't get much thicker than that, he thought. *Oh, the sweet sound of my music.*

"Well, sounds as if you had this planned out for some time actually, Dale. I will get the word out to the families with children. Some may not jump at the offer, but I think your class size will grow with time," the mayor said.

"Understandable, James, completely," Dale said. "I will come back into town next week sometime, so you can see and approve my lesson plans, if you wish to review them, and so we can work out the location. I would like for the classes to start around eight in the morning and go till two. This will give the kids time for their chores and get them home for the afternoon responsibilities as well."

"Sounds good. This has been an interesting day, indeed," James said with a smile.

The men parted with hearty handshakes and claps on the back. Dale and John headed back to the house after a full day of meetings and greetings, shopping, and, in Dale's case, conspiring. They laughed and joked as men do when they are alone. The hot topic of conversation was of course the war, which Dale found intriguing but had no ties to. Even though John lived in the North, his binds had him as a Southerner through and through.

Over the course of the next couple months, Dale earned the trust of everyone in town. He was regarded as a hardworking man with a true interest in teaching children. He was friendly and approachable. He was dependable and committed. He was...a liar and conspirator. A torturer and a murderer, but that would come about soon. Sooner than some would like.

In order for Dale to begin his games, he had to first take over the house as his own. He had his plan, and it was about come to fruition. The families in North Carolina would be his alibi, or maybe the war that was pressing further north.

The South and General Lee just might pull this off, as John had insisted during their conversations. However, when Dale went to town for his class at the Town Hall, which was where it had been decided it would be held, there was mail there with a North Carolina address on his desk. It had become easier for the mailman to just give Dale the mail for the Wolfs, and of course he was trusted.

During the course of the day, Dale made certain to let those around him know that John and his family had received word from home and that he hoped all was well, since it had been such a long time since they had received any word from their families. Dale made a trip to Bill's store and picked up some fabric for Beth. He told Bill about the letter and asked Bill how long it had been since John had mentioned having any communication from his family. Bill thought on this and couldn't remember the last time that John or Beth had heard from home. Dale then stopped by the feed store to pick up some feed, on John's account, of course. Sarah, the daughter of the owner, Benjamin, said she hoped all was well when Dale excused himself from a conversation, stating he had to get back to the house to give Beth the mail, because they had gotten word from Carolina and he didn't want to hold up the news they had received.

"Make sure you come back soon, Mr. Plush," Sarah remarked. She playfully touched his shoulder and batted her eyes.

Dale paused slightly at this, smiled back at her, and assured her he would be back in the near future.

While he was in the stores, Becca waited patiently at the wagon. She wasn't aware of the news Dale was spreading; she did not know of the letter yet.

Once the two of them arrived at the house, Becca rushed inside to tell her mom of the day's lessons. She enjoyed school and she was a very good student. *Was.* Dale excused himself and went to the barn to finalize his plans for the evening. Tonight had been selected by a greater power, and he could not afford to cross that power.

One of his duties around the house had been preparing wood for the upcoming winter. Part of this task was to remove a stump from the ground. He had done this two weeks prior but had decided to leave the hole there and not fill it in, at least not yet... But now the time had come. His biggest obstacle was, of course, not fear or concern, but John. That had to be swift and clean, but he first needed him to write a letter of his own.

Dale took his knife from his pack and changed into his chores clothes, since he had some big chores tonight. He needed to be careful because messes took so long to clean and, even then, there was always a chance that he'd miss something. The barn and the garden were suitable locations, but he would work something out.

***

He walked into the house and handed Beth the mail. The letter from home was on top. He went to get some milk and watched Beth from across the kitchen as she opened the letter with excitement. As she read the letter her reaction was just as he had hoped. His luck was incredible. She began to cry and dropped the letter on the floor. Dale rushed to her and reached her just as her knees gave out. She lay in his arms sobbing as Becca walked in. "What's wrong, Mommy, what's wrong?"

Dale asked her to please leave them alone for a bit, until he could calm her mother down. Becca didn't want to leave but knew it was probably best for now.

Dale reached for the letter and read what it said.

My Dearest Beth,

I am so sorry for you to find out this way, but your brothers have been killed during different conflicts in this war of hate. By the time you receive this, the boys will have been buried and set to rest, but we would very much like to see you and your family if the opportunity exists for you. We have lost so much and it would do our hearts good to see you all. We do understand the danger such a trip would entail but if possible, please come home. I pray for you and your safe travels if you do in fact choose to make the journey.

With all our love,
Mom and Dad

That dirty, sadistic smile creased his lips, and as Beth lay in his arms it all came together. "Beth, I am so sorry for your loss. Why don't you go upstairs and lie down for a spell? I will tend to Becca for the afternoon and you can take some time to work things through."

She nodded docilely and stood up as if in a trance. Dale kissed the letter and placed it on the counter. He went outside and called for Becca. She came around the corner, sniffling and red-eyed from crying. "How is Mama, Dale?"

"Well, sweetie, she is not good, I am sorry to say. She received a letter from home and the news is not good. It's most tragic, actually. But that would be for your parents to tell you. We will do our chores until your daddy comes home. Unless you would feel better if we played a game." How could his luck change now?

"Oh, I guess we could play a game for now. What would you like to play?" Becca replied.

Dale was a little let down by her glumness. He suggested a walk around the house instead of a game due to her mood. Becca liked this idea better. She reached up and grabbed Dale's hand. A hot flash scorched through Dale's body at the sensation of her hand in his. This was the beginning and there was no turning back.

Becca was talking about her mommy and how much she loved her and blah blah blah. Dale slowly reached behind his back and grabbed the handle of the knife. He pulled upward to remove the blade from his pants. He walked with the knife beside him, following the movement of his leg to block the vision of her death sentence from Becca.

He no longer cared for the girl. He had no feelings for her. The only feeling in him now was hot lava coursing through his veins. He began to sweat, but his breathing remained calm. His temperature rose to a simmering level, but he felt cold and lifeless. Becca was still talking as Dale raised the knife straight up from his side, still hiding the steel from her, and then suddenly her words were cut short.

She tried to talk but couldn't. There was water in her throat but she hadn't taken a drink. There was also a sharp pain in her neck, like a big bee sting, only worse, but fading quickly. Now the water was coming out of her mouth and she was choking on it. Dale had dropped her hand, so she turned to him for help, but even her young mind understood Dale was not there to help. She dropped to her knees and grabbed for her throat. The warm wetness mixed with the cold steel. The confusion and fear. The sadness and aloneness. The shock and the horror. No pain though. The light was fading. She then looked up into Dale's eyes and she saw the demon that had been hiding, lying in wait for the chance to strike. His smile showed off the evil beneath his skin. He raised his hand to his mouth, slowly and softly kissed his first two fingers, then leveled his hand and blew the kiss of death toward her. She felt it enter her soul as the lights of her world went out.

Dale stood looking at the blood drain from the small girl. It always amazed him how much blood such a small person contained. The look of confusion and fear and sorrow mixed together in those young eyes. At first they looked at him for help. Then he saw her realize that help was not there before her. Only hate and a coldness that could never be rivaled by anyone but the devil himself. Once Becca fell to the ground and the blood ceased flowing from her poor soul, Dale turned her over to inspect his work. He was very impressed with the precision of the insertion of the blade. Going in on the right side of her neck with the working side of the blade facing the front of her neck, severing the jugular and the vocal box, before coming out the left side of her small, fragile neck. The ironic thing was that he could not remember actually inserting the blade. Only lifting it along his side and then looking at her as she fell to her knees, bleeding.

Dale slowly removed the blade from her neck. Then he wiped the blood from it on Becca's dress. He replaced the knife in its sheath. He leaned over and grabbed Becca's wrist and began to drag her to the garden. For now he needed to move the body from plain view but couldn't risk taking her in the house yet. He got to the garden and decided to lay her between the rows of corn. He looked her small body over one more time, smiled, stretched, and walked to the house. Time to check on Mommy.

***

He entered the house and quickly went to the kitchen to wash his hands in the basin. He didn't get any blood on his clothes, due to stepping away from Becca just as the blade severed the jugular, but he did get blood on his hands. One thing he knew is that the longer the blood sets, the longer it takes to remove. While washing his hands, he looked in a mirror and glimpsed into the eyes of a different soul. The soul was vast, void, dark, evil, and mean, just mean, just evil, pure darkness...and he liked its company.

Dale walked up the stairs and looked in on Beth. She had in fact fallen asleep and seemed to be sleeping well. Dale walked over to the bed, sat on the edge, caressing Beth's hair and face. Then he slid his hand down farther across her breasts and then back to her face. She moved a bit but did not wake up. He took a rope and slid the noose end around one wrist then slipped another around the other wrist. He got up and tied her left hand then walked around the bed and tied the right one. This caused a bigger stir from Beth, but her exhaustion from crying kept her subdued. Dale moved to her legs, smooth and strong, protruding from her dress, and tied each leg to one of the corner posts to the bed. He stood back and looked at his sleeping beauty, lying on the bed in the shape of an X. Dale laughed to himself, "X marks the spot."

Dale walked down to the kitchen and got an apple and some water. He sat on the front porch, where John and he sat that first night. He cut the apple into quarters with his knife, yes, the same knife, and slowly enjoyed the juicy, crisp taste of the apple. He finished his glass of water and walked to the pump to refill it. As he sat down, he noticed the darkening of the sky and realized that John would be coming home shortly. He placed the water on the ground and walked to the garden in the back. He lifted Becca up, put her over his shoulder, and carried her in the house. He took her upstairs and placed her in a sitting position against the back wall, although he couldn't keep her from slumping forward. He turned to the bed and took the fabric out of his back pocket that he had bought that day with the Wolfs' credit. He tied a knot in the middle of the fabric and placed that gently in Beth's open mouth. He then lifted her head slowly and tied off the fabric in the back and then lay her head back down. He sat there for a while longer, and as Beth began to move and open her eyes, he leaned forward, brought his forefinger to his mouth, and made a shushing gesture.

Beth's eyes exploded open and she pulled in all angles against her restraints as her screams were sufficiently muffled. She was breathing rapidly and her chest heaved. Her eyes darted around the room to see what she could, and when she realized there was no help in the room she turned her gaze back to Dale, who sat patiently. She squinted her eyes and cocked her head to the side as if to motion what she couldn't verbalize... "Why, Dale, why?"

"Now don't go trying to understand why this is all happening. It was always going to happen. Timing is everything, and your family provided me with the shout of go with their letter. I am sorry for you and for your losses, but soon you will not have to worry about that emptiness you feel inside. You too will be empty, but for now you just lie there and pray and think of all the good memories while you still can. Don't struggle too much, I know you will try when I walk away, but once you start to bleed I would stop because the burning feeling from the ropes will hurt immensely." He then leaned forward and kissed her forehead softly.

Dale smiled at her, stood up, and walked down the hall to the stairs. Then he was gone. She looked at her legs and the restraints, then to her hands, and knew she would not be able to free herself. So she lay still to conserve her energy. Dale had said she was going to die... *Wait, wait... Where is Becca? What has he done to Becca? Could Dale hurt her?* He had shown such devotion to her. *Could he harm the child?*

She looked out the window to ask God to protect her young Becca and realized the sun was down for the day. John. *Oh, John, please be careful, baby. Oh, John, I am so sorry.* And she cried for what was coming, not knowing what had already happened. If she had known, her heart would have broken right then. If she had known what was to come, she would have screamed herself into a panicked heart attack.

Dale was sitting at the table when John walked through the door. John smiled and said hello and then noticed a change in Dale that terrified him. His heart sank and his breathing increased. He scanned the room quickly. "John, we need to talk about some very important things. Just us men. Please sit down and read the letter that Beth received from her family. Do not ask me any questions. We will get to everything in a minute. Now, sit and read." Dale pointed at the letter on the table.

John stood for moment, looking at Dale. His eyes looked hollow and his face lacked all emotion. He looked dead. John noticed Dale's knife lying beside his arm on the table.

Why is that there? What has he done? What is he going to do? Why...what...why...what has he done? His mind raced.

John stepped closer to the chair. There were three pieces of paper, one of which he could see had been written on, but the other two appeared to be blank. As he grabbed the letter he asked, "Is my family safe? Are they OK?" Then he sat down, but returned his eyes back to Dale and sat there looking at him, hoping for answer he didn't get.

Dale blankly stared at John, then shifted his eyes to the letter, then back up to John. This time he opened his eyes a bit wider and nodded toward the letter. He kept his arms on the table, with his fingers laced in front of him. He sat upright with his arms resting on the oak.

John looked at him questioningly and fearfully. He tried to remain calm and stoic in the face of the man he had come to know as his friend, but the fear for his wife and daughter consumed him. He reached for the letter, maintaining his gaze on Dale. Then he slowly lifted the parchment and dropped his eyes to read the fateful letter. As he read, he was confused and hurt even further. One, he had gotten to know Beth's brothers very well before they married. To have lost them both to this Godforsaken war was hard for him to accept. It would have been even harder on him had it not been Dale, still sitting and staring at him, who had given it to him. What did he have to talk about that was more important than this death notice?

"How is Beth? She was very close with her brothers, Dale. Where is she?" John asked nervously.

Dale was now ready to continue his game. "Beth is hurt deeply due to this news. That is a hard way to learn that those close to you have departed our world for eternity. She is upstairs lying down."

"I want to see her, Dale. Where is Becca? Is she upstairs with her? Does Becca know of the letter?" John was beginning to become impatient.

"Yes, Becca is upstairs with Beth, and no, she doesn't know of the letter's contents. I thought it best to not tell her. We will go upstairs in just a few minutes. You need to take care of two things first, and neither of us are going to leave this table until I'm satisfied." Dale spoke very methodically and punctuated each word as if they were the most important. "I have laid two blank sheets of paper for you to write upon. The first paper is for your response back to Beth's family. You will let them know that your heart goes out to them and you all will be on your way to them as soon as you can get things set up here; someone to watch over the house and the farm. That someone will be me, of course, and my name needs to be in the letter. The second paper is for letting James know what has taken place down South, and you all will be leaving right away to go to her family. You will let him know that you will be gone for some time. You will identify me as responsible for staying at the house, maintaining it, and working the farm until your return. You need to add that while you are leaving me here with some money, I must be allowed to use your credit, and once you have returned you will settle all scores." Dale was nearly finished with his instructions, then thought to add, with a smile, "John, I will be reading these before they are put in the envelopes and sealed for their recipients. If I even *think* you are trying to warn them of something, or if you just outright refuse to comply with these very easy requests, I will enjoy watching you react to your wife bleeding out. Do you understand me?" He was very articulate and calm.

John sat there looking into evil. He couldn't place it at first, but now he could see the hate and dread. He enjoyed what was taking place, and John actually thought Dale would rather him defy Dale just so he could hurt his wife and watch John suffer with each cut, each stab, each scream, and every drop of blood he drained. Beth. Beth. Beth.

What about Becca? Why would he use his wife as the first bargaining tool and not his daughter? Becca's pain would be even greater on him. Maybe Dale figured John would refuse and leave Dale with no choice but to torture and kill his wife in front of him, as proof of what he would do to Becca if the refusal continued. If that was in fact the case, then any refusal would result in the death of his wife, because the real threat would be next; the death of Becca.

John reached for the paper and began to write his reply to Edward, Beth's father. Then he wrote to James and told him of their immediate departure for Carolina because of what had happened. The writing was surprisingly easy and quick. With all the stress he was feeling and the uncertainty of what was ahead, he was eager to move on so he could see his wife and daughter. His beautiful girls. He signed the letter to James and looked at Dale, who seemed off inside his own mind. John was glad he couldn't see what Dale was thinking about. However, if he had seen just a glimpse of this Dale, things may have turned out differently for him and Beth.

John started to stand and Dale shot up out of his seat, grabbed his knife, and stepped toward John so swiftly that John shouted out in surprise and sat back down so hard and fast that he tipped over the chair, hitting his head hard on the floor. The room spun and went from light to dark several times before he regained his grasp of the world. He rubbed his head and looked up into the chuckling face of Dale. Dale offered his hand to John to help him up but then removed the supportive gesture and told John to get up. John stood up and watched Dale as he read the letters. Then John recovered two envelopes and addressed one to Beth's parents and one to James West. John handed Dale the envelopes and requested to see Beth and Becca. Dale placed the envelopes on the table, turned to John, and said, "If you would like to go up and see them, let's go. Walk slowly and do not make any sudden movements. I wouldn't want anything to go wrong. Go on then." Dale said this in a teasing southern drawl.

John waited just a moment then turned toward the stairs and called for Beth and Becca as he started up. He called for them again and broke out in fevered anxiety when he received no reply. He could hear Dale walking up the stairs behind. He turned to him and asked, "Why won't they answer me? What have you done to them?"

Dale's only response was a cold, dry, evil grin, with eyes that seemed to stare into space. Once up the stairs, John turned down the hall toward the far bedroom. He increased his stride, fearing what he was about to see. Maybe it would be fast. Maybe there would be no pain, no sorrow. He entered the room and stopped as he looked at his wife tied to the bed. Legs spread open and tied down, with her arms in the same position above her head. He couldn't believe his eyes. "Oh, my God, baby, are you OK? Where is Becca?" John asked.

Tears were brought on by confusion, love, fear, anger, and the knowledge that none of them were going to live through the night. He had to act now. He could overpower Dale. Now, he had to do it now! He looked down at Beth, winked, and puckered his lips, trying to give her hope. He drew a breath, closed his eyes, visualizing victory, then exhaled and spun to the left.

What was that? his mind screamed. It was there on the floor by the wall. He couldn't quite make it out as he spun, and he had to act fast if he wanted any chance at victory. What was that on the floor? He lowered his head and looked to his right. But what the hell was it? Then he realized, then he knew. He fell to his knees in front of his little girl. He sobbed, breathing heavier and heavier but not getting any air. He reached out and felt Becca's leg. He crawled closer and lifted her head, which made a wet peeling sound. The sound was deafening and John began to convulse, full of emotion. "My poor baby, my poor angel, Daddy is so sorry!" he screamed through his tears. He vomited, then spat, "I am going to kill you for this, you devil! You evil man!"

Dale stood back by the door while John took in the scene of his wife strapped to the bed. John was starting to shake, as was his voice. He figured it wouldn't be much longer until John fought to stay alive, to save his family. Dale took a couple steps to the left and bumped the closet door, hoping to get the reaction he wanted.

At the angle at which John stood, with the moonlight shining into the room, Dale had the opportunity he needed to defeat John. Just then John started to turn around and then he stopped, turned back, and fell to his knees. Dale was all smiles. The sorrow and agony filled Dale's soul with profound ecstasy and satisfaction. So much so, he almost missed his window of opportunity. He was so wrapped up in his own merriment that Dale merely caught a glimpse of John turning toward him, preparing to stand. However, unfortunately for John, that was all that Dale needed.

He placed the knife handle firmly against his stomach and then thrust forward just as John made eye contact with Dale. Just one, double-handed shove was enough to send the tip of the blade into John's neck, followed by the rest of the seven inches of steel until all Dale could see was the handle. Dale took a quick step back, avoiding the blood, and watched with delight as John took several gasping breaths and clawed at the handle, trying to ease it back out, but his hands kept slipping through the blood.

John knew he would see Becca soon and that Beth would catch up with both of them in heaven. He sent out a prayer to heaven for a quick death for his wife. He turned back to Becca, crawled beside her, sat with his back to the wall, pulled Becca over to him, and stroked her hair as the last thoughts left his mind. Dale allowed him that last private moment.

Dale admired the love that was displayed in John's last moments, even if it was all for nothing. He was dead and so was his daughter, but he did love in such a pure and heavenly way, much in the same way that Dale hated in a pure and hellish way.

Dale continued to stare at John until the color had completely disappeared from his face. He reached forward and removed the knife. He did not clean it off this time. Instead, he turned and walk to the edge of the bed. "Sweet, sweet Beth. You have lost so much so quickly. How could you possibly want to live any longer? Your brothers, fighting for their beliefs and snubbed out by the weapons of war." Dale spoke as he stroked her hair with his blade. "Your husband, fighting for his family and taken down by seven inches of steel through his throat." The blade slid down her face, between her breasts, down to her navel, then back up through her breasts to just below her chin. "Your daughter, for being small, weak, and trusting." He finished with a smile and a wink as he drove the shank up and down. Beth's eyes widened, then her entire body went limp for good.

Dale kissed her affectionately and then pulled down on the handle. He leaned over her and cut the ropes holding her arms. He stood, moved to the bottom of the bed, and cut the ropes which held her lifeless feet in place. He stretched his back and realized he was starving. Dale looked around this room of blood, snickered, and strolled downstairs to clean himself up and eat. Damn, he was starving.

***

He finished eating, cleaned the dishes, and walked upstairs. He grabbed John. It was a good idea to deal with the heaviest first. He slung John over his shoulder and carried him outside. He walked around to the back of the house, past the garden, and to the hole he hadn't filled in yet by the stump he had removed weeks ago. He dropped his head and rolled his shoulder so John could slide off easily. The corpse of his host flopped into the hole. Dale took a deep breath, satisfied, and went inside for Beth. After she had been dropped off, Dale went for Becca. He took the sheets off the bed, laid them on the floor, and rolled Becca up inside the sheet. He then carried her to the family plot he had dug out.

Dale walked to the barn, grabbed a can of kerosene, and dumped it over the family. He struck a match, lit the box of matches, and pitched the small fireball into the pit. The fire consumed the hole immediately. He sat down on the grass, enjoying the warmth of the campfire. With the fire and the events of the day and evening, he fell asleep on the lawn.

***

When he woke up, the sun was just beginning to shatter the darkness of the night. The stiffness had settled into his body during his slumber. He rolled over onto his chest, brought his knees up under him, pulled his hands back along the cool, wet ground, and pushed up. With considerable effort, he rose and cracked his back and neck to loosen himself up. Dale looked to his left at the smoke rising up from the hole, and he stepped closer to the edge. When he looked down, he smiled hatefully. Perfect. Just perfect. The bodies had been reduced to mere charred bones. He walked over to the side of the house, grabbed the shovel, and began to fill in the hole, just as he said he would.

Dale finished this task quickly, even though he wished he could bask in the glow of his own greatness, because he had another very important task to complete before he had to be off to school. He walked briskly to the stable, hooked up the wagon to Nell and Storm, and drove them hard to the farm. If someone got nosey around the house, Dale didn't want the wagon and the horses to lead to questions which had no real answer. Once he arrived at the farm he unhooked the horses and set the wagon ablaze. It didn't take long for the wagon to erode to embers, which he raked out smoothly to allow the heat to exit quickly.

Once the embers had died down, he shoveled them into a shallow ditch line he had been digging out, and then covered them. He then turned to Nell, and a dilemma presented itself which he had been trying to avoid. He had never intentionally harmed a domesticated animal and had an actual respect for horses and dogs, the most loyal of animals, or so he thought, anyway. What to do with Nell? Time was running short; he needed to be headed back at the house soon. He would ride Storm back and say that the family left before day's first light for Beth's family home, but Nell could not be at the house or here if the story was to be believed fully, just in case those pesky noses started sniffing around.

He decided to leave her. Dale needed to figure something out in case she was discovered, but he had at least a couple days before people started to suspect something was wrong. "These people here love me, at least for now," he said aloud, which caused a smile to break out on his face. He heeled Storm's sides and headed back to the house.

Once there, Dale knew he was running low on time, but he thought he had a pretty good reason for his tardiness today so he stopped to bathe. He readied himself as he would do any other morning then left for town. He felt sorrow for Storm, who had been on the run all morning, but he would get some rest soon. He went straight to the stables then over to the Town Hall for his class.

James was talking with the children as Dale walked through the door. Dale met James's eyes and motioned his head to the right of the room. James excused himself and asked the children to sit quietly. When James reached him, Dale handed him the envelope and said, "Beth received a letter from home yesterday. Her brothers have been killed in the war. John, Beth, and Becca left before first light to head back to Carolina to be with her family for a while. John wrote this and wanted me to get it to you."

James read the letter, looked up at Dale, looked back down at the letter, refolded it, and put it in his shirt pocket.

He put his hand on Dale's shoulder and said, "Wow, Dale, if you need any help at the house or on the farm, you just let me know. In times like this, it's nice to live in a small town."

Dale lightly smiled, nodded, and responded, "Thank you kindly. We will need to talk about the schooling part after class today. Don't know if I can keep it up every day. The teaching and the work at the house and farm, I mean. May be just a bit too much for me."

A little defeated, James said, "Yes, I suppose that is a good point, but I know there will be plenty of unhappy kids in this room."

James walked away and Dale turned to his class. He explained to them what had happened (well, what he wanted them to think had happened, anyway). He informed the class that with his new responsibilities, the class would need to be put on hold, at least until he could work out a routine. The class moaned with displeasure and a few of the children cried. Whether the tears were for the absence of the Wolf family or for the future absence of Dale, he did not know. But my, were those tears satisfying to him. Pain comes in different forms and this one was good too, because it was pure emotion. He promised that as soon as he could work something out, he would get in touch with all of them.

The day went by at a decent pace, and Dale was exhausted. He went back to the house, stabled Storm, and went to the bedroom to sleep. This was the first time he had been in the room since his party with the family, and a great sense of energy filled him. Almost to the point that he was afraid he may not be able to sleep, but he tossed himself on the bed and assumed the position he had Beth in just a short time before. He slept quickly and soundly.

When Dale awoke it was dark and he was still exhausted. So he undressed and lay back down again. Again he fell to sleep with no trouble and this time he slept until the morning light was pouring into the house.

After eating, Dale worked on the bedroom, cleaning and cleaning. He was resting outside on the porch with a glass of tea when Bill came walking up the side of the house.

"Hello, Dale, how's it going today?" Bill asked.

Dale, nearly choking on his tea, responded, "Well, sir, would be better if I weren't scared into a spasmodic death." He reached out to shake Bill's hand.

The greeting was met matter-of-factly as Bill laughed at Dale's response. This left Dale thinking, *Wow, he isn't here to check on my story. He is here to check on me. I may spare him, just maybe.* This caused a chuckle to escape Dale, which of course Bill took for a response to his own laughter. This caused him to laugh harder.

Once the laughing had ceased, Dale brought some tea out for Bill and they talked for hours, enjoying each other's conversation as much as the tea. Only when Dale said he needed to run out to the farm and look around during light hours did Bill rise and offer his help when needed and left.

Dale did actually go out to the farm afterward. He walked around and got a feel for the place. While he walked around he didn't see Nell. She could have been wandering around somewhere, he supposed, but he had hoped to see her. He had only been to the farm a couple times with John and each time was it was only to grab some feed or hay. The majority of his work was performed at the house. John took care of the farm. But because of the events over the last couple of days, everything was his responsibility. Well, at least to some degree the farm was, but maintaining the house was more important. In case someone stopped by, he wanted to make sure it looked like he was at least trying to maintain the place.

This was the way things went for a little while. Dale really wanted to play with someone else, though. He didn't like it when the games had to be put on hold, even if he knew it was for the best. He stayed the course, however. He kept the house up and worked out on the farm three days a week. Good thing, too, because it seemed like a couple times a week someone was stopping by either the house or the farm. They wanted to make sure he was doing alright. They always offered help too. Everyone sure did love the Wolf family. Dale made a point to have tea ready all the time because of the frequency of the visits from the townfolk. At first he thought someone had figured out what he did. In the end, though, they were coming just to say hello, can we help with something, blah blah blah. Dale hoped, with the approaching winter, the interruptions would decrease greatly.

***

Dale had been spending the majority of his time chopping up wood for the winter ahead. He did not want to be caught at the end of the season without enough wood. So he set to work on harvesting the crops from the garden. He canned them and prepared the land for the next entries. However, seeds weren't going to be planted for next season's harvest. Once the food was taken care of, he concentrated on the woodpile and the trees that John had cut down earlier in the year. They needed to be cut up and sized for the wood stove and the fireplace. This was going to take some time, but he had been slowly working on the wood for a couple weeks. He felt good about his progress, but if he came up a little short he was sure he would be able to trade for some wood with someone in town. Dale also needed to practice shooting the bow. He needed experience if he wanted to acquire meat for his protein during the winter. If he didn't learn to shoot well, he may be forced into cannibalism, and he definitely didn't want things to end up like that. He did have his own morals, after all.

He eventually got to be a pretty good shot and thought the bow and his newfound skill might come in handy with other things in the future. He had a large amount of wood cut to size in two different areas; one for the fireplace and one for the wood stove. He really couldn't imagine using all of the wood, even if they were in for the hardest winter he had ever experienced.

***

Their first snowfall was in early December, and Dale was ready to begin his classes again, not to mention his games. He missed the excitement of both events, teaching and killing. He saddled up Storm and went into town. It had been a couple weeks since anyone surprised him with a visit, so when he walked into Bill's store for some new, warmer pants, Bill bounded around the corner to shake his hand and give Dale a quick hug, punctuated with a couple pats on the shoulder and back. "How are you holding up, buddy?" Bill asked.

"Pretty good, actually. Still haven't heard from John and the girls since they left, but I suppose with the war going on they were slowed down getting south. I hope to hear from them soon. All is well at the house. I haven't been to the farm lately, but I doubt much has changed. How goes things with you and the store, Bill?" Dale responded.

The two men stood and talked for a while then Bill offered up some coffee and a chair to rest. Dale accepted. War, weather, town news, and schooling were the main topics, and hours had passed before Dale knew it. Dale stood, stretched out, reaching the ceiling of Bill's little store. He set his cup on the seat of the chair. Bill stood up and commented on how stiff he had gotten sitting there and stretched as Dale had. The men said their goodbyes and Dale stepped out into the brisk sunshine and walked across the street and down the road a bit to the Town Hall. James, who was sitting at his desk with his feet up reading over some papers, greeted him.

James peered over the top of the papers and put them down once he saw who had entered his office. He slid his feet off the corner of the table and rose to welcome Dale. "How you been, Dale? Hope all is well with you."

"Just fine, James, just fine. I wanted to talk about getting the school running again, at least during the winter." Dale smiled knowingly of the games that were to come to this town.

Dale and James decided that school would be in session two days a week at the Town Hall just as before. Then, for those who wanted extra lessons, Dale would hold classes at the Wolfs' one to two days a week. After that was settled, Dale went to the feed store and placed a few bags on the credit ledger for John Wolf, who of course would never pay that debt, or any debt for that matter. Dale then went home and began to prepare his lesson plans for his upcoming classes.

***

Dale woke up the next day and rode out to the farm. He needed to get some straw and hay for the house, plus he needed to clear his head and ready himself for what was to come.

He was going to unleash the wickedness on this small town. The wickedness he saw when he looked in the mirror. He saw it after ending Becca's short life. It stared back at him blankly, sneering hellish torment that could only be subdued by the games. He needed to play. He needed to play very soon to ease the throbbing, the drumming in his head... the scratching at his soul...the ripping of his heart.

The first step was to remove the law. George Ruthmann was the sheriff of Stevenson and he was pretty much paid to do nothing. The folks of town were very docile and didn't really have use for a lawman, but it was nice to have one just in case. This caused a laugh, an evil, darkening laugh that came from Dale's gut, because he was the "just in case." He was the reason the town's people had wanted a lawman around to discourage wrongdoing. Fights and public drunkenness were the height of the worries these people had. Maybe it wasn't necessary to get rid of George after all. No, George must go!

Back at the house, Dale sharpened his blade as he thought out the plan for Sheriff Ruthmann's dismissal. The sheriff was a lazy, out of shape, overweight, worthless being, but he was good with his six shooter and there was no better hand to hand fighter in the local area, or so Dale was told.

***

George went to Hagerstown every Thursday to check in with his peers and have a few drinks in the saloons. George also enjoyed the company of the working girls. There were no such girls in Stevenson.

The Game Evil Plays

Dale left his house and headed for the crossroads bridge. It was a cold and windy morning, and Dale had to cover up good to keep from getting winter bitten. He had gotten to the crossroads early in order to set up his little trap. He had hooked up the buggy to Storm and added a busted wheel to the back. Dale got to the spot he wanted for his ruse, then took off the good wheel and hid it behind a tree for the time being. Then he attached the broken wheel and waited in the cold morning air for George to come unsuspectingly down the road.

When George did arrive, everything went according to plan, of course... Lately everything had been going that way for Dale. He paused for a minute and thought, *Everything has been going perfectly. When will that come to an end? I must stay on my toes and be ready for anything.* But this wasn't that time for sure.

As George bent over to look at Dale's busted wheel, Dale slid over behind him and brought his knife down hard and fast through the back of his neck, severing his spinal column and rendering him paralyzed. George's arms went limp and he slumped forward before he understood what had bitten his neck on such a cold, cold day.

Dale dragged George over to the side of the bridge, all the while whistling a tune. Dale removed his knife and stuck it into the wooden railing on the bridge. Then he picked up George's head and kissed him above each eye, smiled, and wished him well as he pushed him over the edge of the bridge. Dale stood and looked down and watched as George made contact with the freezing water below. He stood there, watching the sheriff's body float down the river, then turned to his buggy, retrieved the wheel, and replaced it. He then led the horse toward Hagerstown and released it. After that, he turned Storm around toward the warmth of the stable and his house.

***

Dale ate and warmed himself by the fire. Dinner consisted of rabbit and potatoes, with some coffee. The rabbit was his first conquest with his new weapon of choice. So the meal was gratifying for multiple reasons. Once he finished eating and had sat for a spell to rest, Dale bundled back up and headed out for his next game. Dale headed to James's house, where he would find the doors unlocked and the lanterns extinguished for the night. He slipped in and made his way to the back of the house.

James's house was a one level home, with big rooms and a lot of windows to light the way. Down the hall and to the back room on the left, he turned the knob and peered in the door. This was where James's son, Jacob, lay sleeping. He was eleven. Without closing the door, Dale went into the room directly across from Jacob's and found James and his wife lying in bed. Dale had actually never met this woman and didn't remember ever hearing James talk about his wife. Dale walked over to James's side of the bed and slid the blade of his knife across his neck from right to left. James, startled awake, began to thrash around, clutching at his neck. His wife sprang up onto her knees and screamed at the sight of her husband in obvious pain and the figure standing before her... Was the shadow smiling at her? She got up and ran to her son's room and slammed the door on her way inside. She woke Jacob up, opened the window, and helped him crawl through it. She then threw him a blanket. As she pulled herself up onto the window frame and started through it head first, she felt a sharp cut across the backs of her ankles. She let out a scream of pain that was greater than childbirth. Then she was dragged back inside. Just as she was pulled completely into the room, she yelled to Jacob, "Run, baby, run!" Then she was silenced, her words to be heard no more.

Dale ran outside and looked around for Jacob. "Jacob, Jacob, where are you, buddy? It is Mr. Plush. I am here to help. What's going on? Jacob, do you hear me?"

"I'm here, Mr. Plush. Who was that in my house? Is my mommy OK? I'm so scared. Please help me, please!" Jacob cried uncontrollably. He walked over to Dale and enveloped him in a hug. Dale patted him on the head and led him back to his house, where Jacob's parents lay dead.

Once inside, Dale reached forward with both of his hands, grabbed Jacob by the neck, and suffocated the little boy. Dale thrived on the power he felt while squeezing Jacob's neck and watched his eyes roll back in his head. The child convulsed until all movement ceased. Dale relaxed his hands and allowed Jacob's body to fall to the floor. He leaned over, picked Jacob up, and lay him back in his bed. He had already placed James and his wife back in their bed. He walked to the living room and dragged some of the wood out of the fireplace and onto the floor with the poker. He then moved the rocking chair and a couple of chairs from the dining room. Once they were lit, he carried them back into the bedrooms. When the beds caught fire, Dale made his way back to the front of the house and saw that the living room was completely engulfed in flames and they were quickly moving through the house. Dale covered his face and ran out the door. He stood outside, and then made his way to the woods, back to his house. He was in desperate need of more warm food and coffee. He was chilled to the bone.

***

The next day started with a knock on his door. Dale groggily got out of bed, stretched, and walked to the door. He opened it and looked out into the face of a very upset Bill Sampson. "What's wrong, Bill? Looks like you might be sick. Get out of the cold and come over by the fire. I'll get you some coffee. Come on, man, get in here." Bill walked in and Dale led him over to the fire, and then walked to the kitchen to make some coffee. Dale walked back into the living room and asked, "Bill, what's going on? Speak to me, buddy. You're kinda scaring me here."

Bill looked up into Dale's eyes. He was crying. "They all burned to death, Dale. The whole family. James, Betty, and Jacob... Oh, God, that poor little boy... The whole family's gone. The town is devastated. I said I would come here to tell you, but also wanted to get away from the town. It's just horrible, Dale. They were good folks, *damn it!*"

Dale controlled his excitement and returned the gloom he saw in Bill. "My, God, Bill, when did this happen? How did it happen?" he asked.

"Looks like the house was burning most of the night. By the time anyone noticed the fire it was already too late. No one knows for sure how it started, but my guess is a lantern or the fireplace. This time of year, they are the number one and two causes of fire," Bill informed Dale.

Dale excused himself and went to the kitchen to get the coffee, which had started to boil. He poured them each a cup and walked back to the room, handing the coffee over to Bill.

Bill just sat there staring into his cup, looking for answers to life's questions but only finding his warm drink. Dale went to his room and changed out of his winter pajamas and into a pair of pants and a wool button-up shirt. He pulled his boots on and went outside for more wood. After he had a couple small rows stacked inside, he shut the door and sat beside Bill, who wasn't doing very well.

Dale patted him on the shoulder and asked him what he wanted to do. Bill responded by saying he didn't care but he didn't want to go back to town just yet. So when Dale mentioned heading over to the farm and doing some work, Bill said it was fine with him.

Dale had to control himself while they were at the farm. Bill would end up dead like everyone else in town, but Dale really wanted to put that off as long as possible. He liked Bill, well enough to spare him for a few weeks. The main reason, however, was that if too many unexplained events started happening all at the same time, then someone would eventually want answers. One thing Dale didn't want was a bunch of questions and people looking around where they weren't wanted.

***

Dale and Bill headed into town later in the afternoon and went to the remains of the West residence. Bill couldn't bring himself to look at the rubble, but Dale couldn't keep his eyes off it. He was pleased with how well everything had burned and was not worried about anyone being able to identify the inflicted wounds. He walked over to the side of the house, where the bedrooms had been the night before, and looked around on the ground for any evidence that may have been left behind. He saw none.

The town's people were in shock and most didn't want to talk about it just yet. The few that did talk were rambling with horror and fear in their voices. Bill walked up to Dale and asked if they could leave and Dale agreed to go.

They walked back to Bill's store, which was closed, as were all the shops in town, with the exception of the bar. Bill walked to the back of the store and opened a door, where there were stairs leading to his living quarters. Bill showed Dale around his loft of a home. One room just sort of led into the next. His bed was positioned against the far wall on the left and there was a small fireplace on the right, across from his bed. A rocking chair, a table with a couple chairs, and a desk were the only other furniture in the entire place. There was a small room by the sink where Bill's washbasin sat. Bill apologized about the bathroom situation, for the shitter was outside, as was the pump where he got his water.

After a few moments of silence, Dale spoke up and said he was going to head home, but if Bill ever wanted to come to his place he was more than welcome. Bill thanked him and Dale left Bill to his sorrow.

While on his way over to his horse, Dale was stopped by a few men from town he had not yet met. The men didn't bother with greetings. "Teacher man, we were wondering if you had any experience with determining the cause of a fire?" One man spoke up for the group.

Dale paused, drew in a breath of relief, and replied that he did not have any knowledge of how that was done, but maybe the sheriff knew more about the subject.

"Well, we went there first, of course, but George hasn't returned from his trip to Hagerstown yet." They didn't sound very concerned about that.

"I'm sorry, I would love to help but this is really something I know nothing about," Dale said, sounding discouraged.

Then one man spoke up and informed Dale that he was Jason and the other men were Daniel, Joseph, and Patrick. "We all knew James very well and it's hard to imagine he left his fire in such a manner that it would result in this," Jason said as the other men nodded their agreement.

"From what I knew of him, it's hard for me to see that as well. It's possible though that with the snowstorm and the dropping temperatures he overstocked to make the fire last till first light and the wood rolled on him," Dale interjected.

The men thought this through, and Joseph said the very thing had happened to him once, while he was sitting in his living room, but he was able to evade a fire since he was still up. The other men looked at him with amazement and then thought of times in their lives when a disaster had been thwarted because they were not asleep.

After a couple minutes, Dale asked if he could be excused to get home to tend to Storm and the men apologized for holding him up. They all shook hands, saying their farewells, and went their own ways. As Dale rode Storm home, he thought of his next step and knew that he must get to know this group of men. Help where he could and gain their friendship, because this group could be trouble. The one good note was that of the families in town these four were what was left. A couple of farms on the outskirts made up the rest of this very quaint town.

A couple days later, Dale saddled up Storm again and rode into town. He went to Bill's store and stepped inside.

Bill was more than happy to see his friend again. "So I heard you ran into Jason and his crew the other day," Bill started with a trying smile. Dale could tell he was still dealing with the loss of the West family.

"Yes, I did. They inquired as to whether I had any fire investigation experience. How are you holding up, my friend?" Dale asked.

"Well, I am doing as well as can be expected, all things considered. Just watch yourself around them, Dale. They are digging for someone to blame, other than James, of course. I would think that once George comes back to town he will be coming to see you. I wouldn't worry too much, though."

"I look forward to talking with the sheriff, actually. I fear they'd turn their grief in my direction because I'm new around town. I thought it would be good to come to town and let folks see me around some. The talk with the fellows hadn't been sitting well with me, and given what you just told me, I see my feelings weren't misleading me. Thank you for the information." Dale spoke without emotion and really felt no cause of alarm. *I'll just wait for the good sheriff to show up,* he chuckled to himself.

Dale stayed at Bill's for a good portion of the day and spoke neighborly to the few patrons that entered Bill's shop. He received good-natured responses but no sustained talks, which, of course, was understandable, and that's the way he wanted it anyway.

Dale told Bill he was thinking about heading into Hagerstown himself. Thought that maybe it would be better for him as far as a teaching job once the Wolfs came home. "I will stay, of course, until then, but it would be good to get my name around town if something should become available." He asked Bill to hold his mail for him and he told Bill where he would be, in case anyone came asking. He thought of staying there for a couple days to look around and talk to some town leaders for possible positions. Of course, he wasn't going to be staying in Hagerstown, but that wasn't for Bill to know.

***

Dale went home, packed his bag with some clothes, and loaded up Storm for the ride into town. After a couple hours, Dale could see the town on the horizon. He checked into the Hagerstown Inn and then went to the pub for a good steak and some ale. He talked with as many people as he could and introduced himself to everyone with a hearty smile and strong shake. He wanted to instill a vivid memory for those he encountered so when inquisitions were made in the future, those he talked to would remember the teacher from Stevenson. Dale also inquired about jobs with everyone he talked to and learned about a couple seasonal jobs once spring came.

That night, after the town was still, Dale snuck out of town on Storm and rode into the woods that skirted his game town. His life-sized chess match. He then tied off Storm in a shed and headed off to play his next game. The other player was to be Jason, trouble-maker number one. Dale had asked all the right questions when speaking with Bill earlier, and Bill had been so gracious in his explanation of where each member of the crew lived. Really, at some point, things were going to come undone for Dale, but until then he was going to ride it out.

As Dale approached Jason's house, he noticed a light coming from a window on the upper level. The light was not moving, so Dale figured the operator was either getting ready for bed or reading. He pulled some jerky from his pocket and chewed on it until the light was extinguished a short time later. He stood and moved all his joints to loosen them up. He then removed his knife from its sheath and stealthily made his way inside. Warmth filled his soul, and he felt relief instantly attack his fingers and face. He slowly walked up the stairs, which creaked with each step he took. He would be surprised if he made it to the top of the stairs without alarming Jason. However, he did in fact find himself at the top with no guests present. As he slid his feet across the floor to decrease the creaking sound, he realized no one was alert to his presence because the couple was having sex and the steel-framed bed was making enough noise to drown out the sounds just outside their door. He checked the other rooms and found no other person. So he sat down on the bed in one of the other rooms down the hall and waited for the two lovers to finish their dance.

Dale took his boots off, walked over to the railing by the stairs, and tossed a boot over the edge then backed into the room, into the shadows.

"Stay here and be quiet!" he heard Jason whisper to his lover. Then Jason's shadow filled the hall as he looked over the railing and peered down the stairs. Dale hopped out of the room quickly and quietly and pushed Jason over the railing before Jason could register the noise of his movement.

Jason felt hands on his back; his feet lost their connection to the floor and gravity pulled him down. He didn't see the assailant but knew it was the teacher man who had pushed him. If he survived this fall he was going to kill that teacher. However, due to how Jason was doubled-over the railing and because Dale pushed him unexpectedly, Jason hit the stairs with the full force of his weight headfirst, snapping his neck like a small twig. SNAP!

Dale walked down the stairs as the woman began to yell for Jason. Now hadn't he told her to be quiet? But, of course, her yelling Jason's name over and over and asking if he was OK helped hide Dale's footfalls on the steps. He picked up his boot and put his cold foot back inside the warm leather and stood back from Jason for a few minutes, checking for movement, but there was none. Dale went outside and waited for the girl to come downstairs. He knew she would, it was only a matter of time. No one could just wait around and not check things out.

When Dale heard the scream he was waiting for he headed for the woods, humming a lively tune.

Dale got back to the inn in Hagerstown, settled Storm down in the stable, and slipped into his room, quickly going to sleep due to exhaustion.

After Dale bathed and ate, he set out to find the town hall or the courthouse. Either would work just fine. He walked through the door of the courthouse and ran into Judge Remmy, literally. The judge was on his way to the barber shop and was fumbling with some papers. He didn't see Dale standing there, reading signs to see which way he needed to proceed. Both men picked themselves up and looked at who had floored them then began to laugh. My, how times had changed.

Dale accompanied the judge to his haircut and decided on one himself, as well as a shave. The judge invited Dale to lunch and he accepted. They sat eating their sandwiches and chips, talking about possible employment for Dale. Samual, the judge, said he felt very strongly about Dale finding some work in town. He was also pretty certain that a teaching job wouldn't be that hard to find either. The town was growing and kids were a part of that growth. Dale was supposed to come back into town in a few weeks and talk to Samual once he had a chance to speak with the school board folks. Dale thanked him, more for the talk than the help in finding him a job. This was his alibi—he now had a judge to back up his story.

Dale enjoyed his time in Hagerstown that day, checking out the shops and drinking in the pubs. He sat down at a table in the early evening and played a game of poker with some of the other customers in the bar. Then, after a good-natured game, losing money intentionally again and again, he headed off to bed. He didn't go to bed, though. He headed to Stevenson, where Daniel waited, unbeknownst, as his next quest.

***

Daniel lived in a small shack by himself. His wife had died five years earlier of smallpox and he had never remarried. Daniel had been a good husband. And he was a good friend, as well as a good Christian. To make a living, he did small jobs around town for people. Dale didn't know any of that and none of that would have mattered to him anyway.

Dale entered Daniel's house and found him sleeping on the floor, just inside the door. The smell of whiskey was strong, almost nauseating. As he moved around Daniel's body he kicked a bottle, which clanked loudly then smashed against the wood stove, breaking into a hundred pieces. Dale winced and stared at Daniel, who didn't move an inch. Dale kicked him lightly with the tip of his boot and still no movement, just a grunt. Dale sheathed his knife, leaned over, grabbed Daniel under the arms, and picked him up with some struggle. Dale was not a weak man by any measure, but Daniel had hard muscle from his long days of manual labor, and the dead weight didn't help matters. Once Dale had him up, he took a couple choppy steps forward, paused, then threw him down as hard as he could. As Daniel's head bounced off the wood stove, Dale heard a distinct cracking sound as Daniel's skull cracked against the hard metal. With that, Dale turned and walked out of the shack.

Dale considered stopping by Joseph's next. His time at Daniel's was much less than he initially figured. *Thank you, Daniel.* Dale mounted Storm and decided to head back to Hagerstown. He did not want to rush his plan, and he figured he could use a good night's sleep. And he was right; he slept longer this night than he had in weeks.

***

The next day Dale woke to snow, a good foot or so. He was discouraged by the weather but hoped it would not call off his games for the night. If it did then he would look for a different game partner in Hagerstown. The snow did stop shortly after he had breakfast but with as much snow as they had, he figured it would be too easy to track his steps. He called off the games and used the time to think about his next moves some more. A good player always knows his next three to four moves. Always good to stop for a bit and let life return to normal for a while then start back at it. So he left the inn and headed home.

It was freezing inside the house so he quickly started a fire. It took a couple of hours and plenty of wood, burning both the wood stove and the fireplace. As Dale was washing his clothes, a knock came at his door. He opened the door and smiled when he saw Bill standing there. Dale motioned Bill inside. "Come on in, buddy. It's good to see you. Have you been keeping an eye out for me, or you just lucky I was here tonight?" Dale said excitedly. He reached out for a manly shake.

Bill looked grim, but shook Dale's hand and responded sickly, "Well, everyone has been asking where you were at... well, those still alive. Our little town has come across a bad stretch, and you seem to be the one folks are blaming, I hate to say." Dale looked shocked but listened with pleasure. "I keep telling people that you were in Hagerstown, and a couple of the men even came here to look for you yesterday and this morning. I guess you could say I got lucky with you being here tonight but things are getting hostile in town, and all of it is focused on you, my friend," Bill nervously reported.

"Well, now, Bill, it all makes sense for them to be feeling that way, but I must say I am confused. You said 'who's still alive.' What do you mean, Bill? Your tone and body language don't look good. Who else has died since I have been gone? Here, Bill, drink some coffee and warm up a bit. Tell me as much as you know." Dale couldn't wait to hear his games portrayed through the words of an onlooker.

Bill sat down finally, drank some of the coffee, and began his tales. He spoke with the look of terror in his eyes and despair in his voice. He described each scene of death to Dale, and Dale was not disappointed. Bill could be a great reader of the macabre, with the dread and angst that coursed through each word, seeming to know when exactly to pause to create the perfect picture. As Dale listened, his heart leapt with proud ownership. Oh, how he was going to hate killing Bill.

"Bill, I would think each one of these deaths can be explained rationally, without the community blaming me for simple accidents. Tragic, yes, sad, yes, murder...no. By me... Hell no. What do you believe, Bill? Do you think I had anything to do with these terrible events?" Dale inquired.

"Dale, no, not at all." Bill looked lively for the first time that night. "I'm just letting you know what the group is saying and thinking, so you're prepared either when you come to town or when they come to you."

"OK. It would pain me if I thought you figured me to be a part of all this," Dale remarked.

Dale went on to tell Bill that he would be going to town the next day. He said he felt he needed to answer what questions he could and to step out in front of the issues, instead of sitting back and waiting. Just wasn't his style. Which it really wasn't, but Dale wanted to see the effect he had created in town. He wanted to see and hear the fear he was striking in the hearts of the simple citizens of Stevenson.

Oh, how he loved the games he played.

***

Then the two talked of Dale's visit to Hagerstown and how the shop was going for Bill. The weather was mentioned briefly, but the South's advance north and the probable movement into Maryland or even farther was looking more and more realistic. Neither of the men had a stake in the war. Either side could win or lose, but who really thought the South could be so resilient and aggressive? Dale offered Bill a place to stay for the night and he accepted. Bill was worn out from the increasing stress, and the relief that Dale had nothing to do with any of it was so great that he had no energy to go out in the cold darkness of the night. So he slept on the bed in the extra room upstairs, which was Becca's former sleeping quarter.

Dale looked at the ceiling as he lay in bed, thinking about the conversation he and Bill had earlier that day. The town was scared, nervous, and starting to split. This was absolute perfection in his mind. He would go to town tomorrow and smooth some of the folks over, but others would probably not give in so easily. Those would be the next players in his one-sided game. No one else seemed to be having the fun he was and that was just how he liked it. Perfection.

Dale was up before Bill and started cooking some eggs, bacon, and, of course, coffee. How he loved his coffee. Bill walked into the kitchen as the bacon was crisping and the eggs were frying. Dale heard Bill coming down the stairs and poured him a cup of coffee. Bill nodded, took a sip, and nearly dropped the cup. "Wow, that's hot stuff!" he exclaimed.

Dale snickered and turned the eggs.

They had their breakfast, and Dale informed Bill he still intended to go into town and meet some of the accusations head on. "By going into town, maybe I can get through to some just by showing that I'm not going to hide in the shadows, which is what some expect me to do." Bill didn't agree but, in the end, he did understand why Dale felt he needed to do this.

The looks started as soon as they came across the first person, which was Benjamin, the owner of the feed store. Sarah was inside, looking out of the big bay window and… did she just wave? Benjamin, however, did not. He stood tall and broad-shouldered, then crossed his arms and stared at Dale. He shot a disgusted glance at Bill, but only briefly. Dale almost became unnerved by the look in Benjamin's eyes. Solid, stoic, even heroic, which was not a good combination for Dale. Regardless of what happened the rest of the day, Benjamin had to be handled first.

"You are not welcome in this town, stranger. I know I can't keep you from coming in and out of town, but I can keep you from coming into my store. So you best just stay away from me and my family. When George comes back we will get someone to look into what has happened here, and *if* they can prove to me that you had nothing to do with anything that has transgressed here, then I will give you the heartiest of apologies. Now, both of you, move on," Benjamin said in a steady, thought-out speech. He was not scared and he was not nervous. Man to man, one on one, Benjamin knew he could handle Dale, and so did Dale.

"I'm sorry you feel that way, Benjamin. I was hoping to talk with you about the very apparent accidental deaths that have befallen this quaint village, unfortunately, soon after I arrived," Dale began, but Benjamin put his hands up and responded immediately.

"The tongue of the devil is smooth and the words paint a work of art, but thy teeth are sharp and thy mind is rotten to the core... Move on, devil, for I know who you are," Benjamin preached.

Dale smiled and nodded, then heeled Storm to move forward. As he strode away, he looked back to the window and Sarah stood smiling... Then she puckered a kiss.

Dale and Bill rode down the road to Bill's place and headed inside the store. They did not go upstairs, at Dale's request, not Bill's. Bill was all for Dale going back to his house, well, the Wolfs' house, to wait things out. Dale said he was going over to the pub and asked Bill to come along. "Just don't want anyone starting anything when it's their word against mine, is all." Bill said he would go along and so they left the store and headed to the pub.

The pub was a good place for food, whiskey, and conversation. The building was a three-story wood structure. The first floor had a nice, big oak bar with shelving behind it that held the glasses and mugs. A big five-foot by seven-foot mirror was between the two columns of shelving. There were ten round tables with chairs stationed around them. At the back of the room there were stairs that led up to the two levels of rooms.

Today's conversation was all about Dale and the deaths in town, and they didn't stop when he walked in. The bartender, Michael, did a classic double take and about fell over. Anibelle and Stephen were sitting at the bar with their backs to the door. They didn't realize Dale and Bill were standing two feet behind them. "Well, all I have to say is if Dale the teacher man tries anything with me, I will..."

"You will what? I'm curious. If I try what with you? Anyway, I'm not into boys." Dale surprised them both.

"I, uh, I, uh...I didn't say you liked boys... I, uh..." Stephen stammered.

Dale chuckled, "Look, I understand how everything looks. I'm new to town, people start dying, and it makes sense that I would be looked at first. But look at the facts of each situation, at least from what I have heard from Bill. So if something I say is wrong, please let me know."

He explained that each accident was just that, an accident. A fire, a fall down the stairs in the middle of the night, and too much to drink. Then there was the fact that Dale wasn't

The Game Evil Plays

even in town during all of this. He was in Hagerstown and he had plenty of witnesses and folks he talked to and ate with, played poker with, and, oh, yes, let's not forget the ace in the hole...Judge Remmy.

The group was looking between Dale and Bill and each other. Dale bought his audience a drink and sat calmly and talked methodically to make it easier to believe what he was saying. Actually, he almost convinced himself he didn't do anything wrong, so he had to reassure his heart and mind that he had in fact committed the crimes. *Whew*, he felt better now.

They all talked until it grew dark and each member of the gathering had a little too much to drink (OK, maybe way too much, but who was counting?).

Michael was the first to apologize to Dale and said if he heard anyone talking ill of him he would set them straight. Anibelle and Stephen agreed and actually felt stupid for believing Dale had had any part of the accidents... Definitely accidents, not murders. Afterwards, everyone said their goodbyes. Once outside the pub, Dale said it was time for him to get to bed. Bill said that sounded good to him and they bid Michael a farewell.

Dale and Bill made it to Bill's with a fair amount of side-stumbling steps, with their arms around each other, and leaning. Talking and singing loudly, they both missed the young, soft, and quiet voice calling for Dale, hurrying in the cold to catch up to them. Once inside the shop, Bill headed for the steps when he heard the front door open. Bill and Dale turned to see Sarah closing the door behind her. She smiled and said hello to Dale. Then Sarah asked, "Dale, may I talk to you for a minute?"

"Yes, of course, we can," Dale replied.

Bill seemed neglected by this but was too drunk to care and went upstairs saying something about Benjamin finding out and breaking something...

Dale walked over to Sarah, and as he reached her she wrapped her arms around his neck and placed her lips on his. Dale did not resist, not at all. Sarah was young, nineteen, and extremely pretty; dark hair, dark eyes, and thin but with a muscular build. When she cut off the kiss, she said, "My dad wants to kill you and I want you. I plan on getting what I want first." She reached down and grabbed him, lightly squeezing, while rubbing her hand up and down his crotch. She smiled devilishly and her eyes sparkled with sin. Dale didn't normally feel aroused in this way but because of the whiskey and his pure delight in fooling everyone, he was as ready as he was ever going to be. He pushed her up against the wall and put her hands above her head, then lifted her shirt up over her head and undid her skirt and pushed them down. He lightly caressed her from her neck to her power place. He couldn't take the anticipation anymore, so he turned her around, pulled his pants down, and slid inside her from behind. She moaned loudly and writhed against him, reaching back and pulling him farther into her. He turned Sarah around again and pinned her up against the wall, continuing their sexual act.

They lay on the floor afterwards, Sarah draped over him like a blanket, when suddenly she said, "I will kill my dad for you. I will. All you have to do is say so and it will be done."

"I don't think that will be necessary, Sarah," Dale insisted.

"If my dad says he wants to kill you, then that's what he wants, and what he wants he usually gets. If I don't do it by surprising him, you may not be able to defend yourself against him."

"Well, then, I suppose you should take him out while you can," Dale said absently.

"OK, I will do it for you, for us. Will you be able to hide me in your house?" she asked

"OK, yeah, sure. Once you've done whatever it is you do, just come over to the house and I will find a place to hide you. Write a letter confessing to the murder, though, or the township will just add this one to me. Also put in the letter that you're leaving town because you can't live in the house where he used to touch you inappropriately."

"That's perfect. You're perfect. We are perfect together." She sighed.

Dale told her she should leave and they both dressed. He walked her to the door, where they kissed and parted ways. She snuck back home and he went upstairs and slept on the floor. As he drifted off that cold, cynical smile creased his face. He licked his lips, lightly chuckled, and slept. But not peacefully.

Dale dreamt unsteadily for the first time that he could remember. In this dream he was stalking a young boy in his house, teasing him with the death that was sure to come. For some reason, however, the boy didn't fear him. He actually seemed to enjoy the game Dale was playing with him. Why? Why wasn't he scared? He should be fearful; he should be screaming and crying... But he...he was laughing at him!

Dale rose quickly, sweating and panting. He wiped the sweat from his forehead and face and looked around the well-lit room. It was morning, so thankfully he didn't have to go back to sleep. He couldn't take that dream again right now, not ever, as a matter of fact.

Dale stood and looked to the bed and saw that Bill had already gotten up, so he went downstairs. Bill was walking around the store, taking inventory of his items. "Good morning. How did you sleep, buddy?" Bill asked as he made tick marks on his sheet, counting out his supply of black buttons.

"I've had better dreams. You're up and at it early today," he commented with a dry throat. He scratched his head and the stretched out his arms above his head.

"Inventory needs to be done. I have to place another order in a couple days. Boring, deadly work, but it does need to be done, unfortunately," Bill answered.

Dale walked outside into the cool morning air, relieved himself in the outhouse, and filled a jug with water from the pump. He walked back in the store and informed Bill he was going to head home. "I am going to let last night's talk at the bar filter through the town for a couple days. Once it does, maybe the bad blood will ease up and I will come back."

"Yeah, that's a good idea. Let folks chew on what they hear and we will see how it ends up. You know I'm in your corner, and I will do what I can to help sway folks to the good side," Bill said with a caring smile.

Dale got home, started a fire, and then bathed. It felt good to sit in the hot water and wash that nasty dream away. He thought about Sarah—not about the sex, but what she had in mind for her father. More importantly, though, what was he to do with her? Could he use her for his games or was this going to be a one-time affair? Dale thought on this until his water cooled off and then he stood up, stiffly. He must have been in the tub longer than he thought.

Dale went about doing the chores around the house; bringing wood in, cleaning up his dishes, cleaning the house, and general straightening up. He worked until dark then prepared for bed. It was an early night for him, and he hoped he would have better dreams. Like most things since he had come to Stevenson, that worked out for him, and he slept peacefully.

***

The next day, more snow fell. Dale went out to the stables, fed Storm, and groomed him. He talked to Storm about his plans, so he could hear how they sounded out loud. He realized how much he liked them. It excited him to hear such a well worked-out plan, with little room for failure. Knowing he had come up with it excited him even more and, most importantly, he was going to see it through to fruition.

Later that night, Benjamin was sitting by the fire reading *Great Expectations* by Charles Dickens. He enjoyed his time at home, relaxing by the fire and reading. He liked that reading gave him the opportunity to get away from the stresses of his life and allowed him to dive into the characters' lives. When he read, he was literally in another world, often not hearing when Sarah asked him a question. Tonight, that would be his downfall.

Meanwhile, Sarah sat in her room, brushing her hair, staring into the mirror, and thinking of Dale. He was absolutely amazing in every way. She let out a smiling, dreamy sigh and placed her brush down on the bureau. She watched in the mirror as her mood and her face changed from sweet and charming to despicable and conspiring. She knew her dad was sitting in his chair reading by now and other than while he was sleeping, this would be the best time to act out her sadistic intentions. She closed her eyes and envisioned Dale holding her in his arms, telling her she did a good job and that he loved her very much. She wrapped her arms across her front and gave herself a hug to emulate the feeling she wanted. She opened her eyes, dropped her hug, and reached down for the ax leaning against her bureau, then started for the stairs. She stopped at the top of the stairs, the base of the handle in her left hand and the middle of the handle in her right, with the head of the ax up by her right shoulder. Sarah was taught at an early age how to carry and use an ax, for cutting wood, of course, not for her twisted intentions tonight. "I love you, Dale," she whispered. Then she took the stairs one step at a time.

Benjamin was wrapped up in Pip, Stella, Miss Havisham, and Uncle Joe as Sarah made her way across the room. He was smiling as he read, like he usually did, when the ax came down hard through his skull, killing him instantly. The book fell to the floor, and Benjamin's hands fell to his side as his body listed to the left then slowly slid forward off the rocking chair. He lay there in a clump on the floor, his blood spilling out quickly, spreading across the wood floor.

Sarah was in awe at how quickly it all happened. The splitting sound of her dad's skull when the blade broke through was unnerving. It sounded like a watermelon does when it isn't cut all the way through and you have to split it with your hands the rest of the way. She also couldn't believe how quickly his blood drained from his body. She went back up to her room, grabbed the note, and her packed clothes. She placed the note on the counter in the kitchen and then stepped out into the cold, dark air.

***

Dale was rocking in his own chair and sipping some whiskey when the front door opened and Sarah walked in, shivering.

He stood swiftly and went to her. She dropped her bag and engulfed him in her arms. "I did it, baby, he's dead. I left the note, and here I am!" Sarah exclaimed. She was breathing heavily and shook uncontrollably from the cold that had sunk into her bones and shattered nerves. Dale rubbed her back and whispered in her ear, "I love you." It sounded just like she had imagined it.

"Oh, Dale, I love you, too!" she exclaimed. Her eyes watered because of the cold. Otherwise, she would have seen his knife in his hands as he stood up from the chair.

Dale backed away slightly to look her in the eyes. Then he coldly stated, "I didn't say I loved you, Sarah. I said 'I am sorry.'" He saw the realization hit her as the words left his mouth. Her happy, elated expression changed to confused, abandoned, and broken-hearted. Then to understanding, painful understanding as the metal punctured her side time after time. She cried out in agony and fell forward into Dale's arms. She raised her head and said, "I love you," and kissed her prince one last time. Dale let her drop to the floor, then brought the knife down again and again and again, until her lifeless eyes gaped up at him.

Dale picked Sarah's body up, carried it outside, and placed it in the barn behind a row of hay bales. He went back into the house, studied the floor, and realized that her clothes and heavy jacket acted like a sponge and soaked up the blood that ran from her wounds. However, the cleaning took some time due to the amount of blood loss from Sarah's wounds. Once Dale finished, he went upstairs for some sleep. Tomorrow would be exciting and he wanted to be fully rested for the circus.

***

Dale was not disappointed when he entered town a little after noon. Bill was walking across the street to his shop from the pub when he spied Dale tying off Storm to the post at the shop. Dale looked around and smiled, took a deep breath, and then saw Bill jogging over to him. Dale threw his hand up in a wave; Bill responded with a quick hand raise, but it wasn't exaggerated like Dale's. "Come on, buddy, inside, so I can tell you what has happened now," Bill said, slightly out of breath.

Bill walked over to the small wood stove, stoked the fire, and threw a couple more pieces of wood on. Dale said, "Looks like the town is in an uproar. What happened?" He sat down on the rocker.

"Oh, my, it's... Well, it's... Do you want some coffee? I need some before I can go on," Bill asked, and Dale nodded.

With simmering coffee in hand, Bill regaled the tale to Dale. He started with the feed store not opening, then moved on to Stephen going to check on Benjamin and Sarah, then Stephen walking in to the most disturbing sight he had ever and hoped would ever see. The ax was still in Benjamin's head, which was split like a melon, and the dried blood had spread out across the floor. But, God, the smell, the smell was too much, and Stephen admitted to vomiting in the kitchen sink. That's when he saw the letter sitting on the counter and he couldn't believe what he read.

Throughout the story, Dale listened to Bill wonderfully orate the events as an excited fever overtook his body. He was so giddy he slightly shook, like when the cold was a bit much for his skin. Bill saw this as he talked, but dismissed it as a cold chill.

Once Bill was done, he looked like he was going to cry. "So she said that her dad was making her have sex with him?

She had too much and just couldn't take anymore, so she put an ax through his skull? Poor girl... But she could have just left without killing the man," Dale suggested, trying to sound disgusted.

"Well, I wouldn't presume to know how a girl dealing with that kind of thing would react. To live with that, for however long it all went on, must have been trying. I think he deserved the ax, personally, but that is just me," Bill said, defending her actions. Dale had hoped this would happen.

The doorbell rang as Anibelle and Stephen walked into the shop, looking very somber. Anibelle addressed both men as Stephen continued to look for something on his boots, or so it seemed. "We are leaving town, and I do think it will be for good. Too much death, too much sickness, too much evil for this area for it to ever fully recover. We wanted to know if you wanted to come with us, Bill. We were going to stop by John's place to see if you wanted to come too, Dale," she said, disheartened.

Bill and Dale looked at each other for a moment. Dale spoke up first. "I believe I will stay at the house, but thank you for thinking of me. I would just feel bad leaving the house after John entrusted me with his homestead."

Bill looked around the store, thinking. "What would I ever do without all this? Find a store in Hagerstown and sell it all to them, start up another store? Never thought I would ever consider this. Dale, what do you think I should do?"

"Bill, that is for you and only you to chew on," Dale said. His mind raced, thinking of the game. "How about this? How about the three of you come over to the house this evening and we can all talk about it?"

Everyone liked the idea and the dinner date was made. Dale excused himself so he could return home to prepare the meal. When Dale walked out, he noticed how little activity there was. Had he really succeeded in eliminating most of the town? Time flies when you are having fun!

***

Dale stabled Storm, brushed him down, and then fed him. He walked to the back of the house where, under the remaining snow and now compacted dirt, the first family who played his game in Stevenson lay. He stood there and replayed all the events that had led to this day; the sights, the sounds, the emotions, the joyful feeling, and *winning*.

***

Stephen, Anibelle, and Bill showed up together and sat around the table with coffee and water in front of them. After the greetings had taken place, a silence overtook them all, which Dale expected. He figured none of them would know where to start. He finished making dinner and they slowly ate. Well, Dale slowly ate; the others just picked at the food and pushed it around their plates. Dale put his fork down, slid the plate forward, took a sip of coffee, and started. "OK, folks, let's get started because what needs to be talked about is causing some tension here, so let's get it out." He took another drink and asked, "Stephen, are you OK, my friend? I know you have seen an unimaginable scene of macabre and I worry for your mind."

Stephen sat silent for a minute, then spoke for the first time since reliving the experience to Anibelle. "I just can't seem to get that vision out of my head. It doesn't matter what I try to think about. I always end up seeing Benjamin laying on the floor, body unnaturally folded up, with the ax protruding from his head... And all the blood... All that blood." He broke down and started to cry into his hands.

Anibelle reached over to him, placed her hand on the back of his neck, and looked at Dale with incriminating eyes. "Why would you ever ask him to go through that again? Have you no heart at all?"

"Now, Anibelle, I didn't ask him to say all that. I simply asked him how he was doing, because I care. He shared all that because he wanted to. He needs to get it out so he can attempt to move on. See, it doesn't matter if you move away from here if he takes with him those images. He needs to leave them here. I am sorry he hurts so badly, but sometimes feeling the pain is the first step to releasing it."

Bill seemed to understand and spoke up. "I agree, and I have come to understand that if I am to move to Hagerstown or Frederick, I need to leave the ghosts of Stevenson in Stevenson. I plan on leaving once I get everything sold to a shop in Hagerstown. I am going to pack up the store and take it into town and see what I can get for it all and start over doing something else," he said deliberately.

The group sat there for a minute taking in what had been said, and Stephen cleared his throat and said he would help Bill pack and they could all leave together. Anibelle quickly added her name to the volunteer list. Dale commented that if that was the way things were to go, he would assist in any way he was needed.

Bill thanked them all and again the group fell silent.

Later that night while lying in bed, Dale thought out his game and it all seemed to be going well. The little group trusted him, which would cause their demise. Trust was a requirement for a strong bond but if gained falsely, it could be the tragic flaw to ending one's life.

***

When Dale arrived in Stevenson the next day, Bill wasn't the only one beginning to pack up. Michael had started to pack up his bottles and barrels onto his wagon. He told Dale he didn't see how he could stay with everyone else in town running from the bad luck that had struck them all. He said that a few of the farmers from the outlying areas had been into town that morning and once they learned of what had transpired, they too were going to find a different location to gather their supplies. Now the town basically consisted of Stephen, Bill, Anibelle, Michael, and Dale.

Dale left Michael to his packing and walked over to Bill's. Stephen and Anibelle were there already, marking boxes that had been neatly packed previously. They all talked for a minute and Dale found out how things were being done then started to help. The four of them packed nonstop for hours. Then Bill said he had arranged a dinner over at Michael's pub for everyone, so they stopped packing and headed over to the pub together.

The five of them enjoyed a wonderful steak and potato dinner. Since they had already discussed just about everything necessary, not much was said during dinner. Afterward, Dale said he would help Michael clean up if the other three wanted to go back to Bill's. Michael and Dale began to pick up the plates, and Michael poured some hot water in the sink and began washing the dishes while Dale finished clearing off the table. As Dale carried over the dirty dishes, Michael thanked him for the helped. No thanks were needed, but he was about to find that out.

Dale walked back to the table, stacked up the rest of the dishes, and walked them back to the kitchen. Once they were securely on the counter, he picked up the knife that Michael had just set aside to dry. It was very sturdy with a big blade sharp enough to cut through a thick country T-bone steak. It almost surprised Dale at how swiftly and effortlessly the steel slid into Michael's kidney. Michael jolted and spun to face Dale before Dale could remove the blade from his body. Bewilderment, fear, anger, and surprise filled Michael's eyes. He reached out for Dale, but Dale had already stepped back and had removed his own knife from its hiding place. Dale smiled at Michael and said, "You should see how stupid you look right now. Well, come and get me, come on," he teased his victim.

Michael reached behind him to remove the knife and said, "You are the devil. You did it all, didn't you? I may die tonight, but I will send you to hell first!"

Dale raised his face to the ceiling and laughed in an exaggerated and deliberate way. Then he stopped, slowly lowered his head till his chin about rested on his chest, and peered at Michael. "Well, you have figured two things for sure... I am the devil and I did do it all, but, my dear friend, you will not be the one to stop me."

Michael lunged forward, but all he caught was Dale's knife with his stomach. The pain caused him to double over, which sealed his impending doom. Dale quickly pulled out the blade and sunk it into the back of Michael's neck. Michael dropped to the floor, dead. Warmth left his body as quickly as his blood.

Dale stepped over the body and washed his hands and knife. He walked outside and crossed the street. The bell announced his entry as he opened the door, and he looked around to see the advancements the trio had made while he played with Michael.

The group began to grow tired, and it wasn't too long before the white flag was waved on the packing. They grabbed some drinks and sat around the wood stove. They drank and talked for a half an hour or so. Bill headed up to bed, and then Anibelle said it was probably time for them to leave as well. Dale offered to walk them home, and Stephen said that the neighborly gesture was not needed but appreciated. Dale nodded and walked them to the door. Once they were headed down the road, Dale slipped out the front door and quietly followed from afar. They walked to a quaint little home, where Stephen walked to the side of the house toward the outhouse and Anibelle went inside. Dale went to the door of the house.

He opened the door and stepped inside. He walked through the main room and looked into the kitchen, when he heard noises coming from the room to the right. The door was opened, and Dale could see Anibelle changing clothes. He walked in the room and he startled Anibelle badly, causing her to let out a scream. "That won't be the last of those tonight, I assure you, girl. The time has come to play a game. You get to watch first, then you get to play." Dale eerily smiled and walked toward her.

She screamed for Stephen. She flailed wildly at Dale, hoping to catch him with one of her swings, but Dale simply put his hand up to block and brought his other hand up, which held the knife. He caught her arm with it and cut it badly. Blood began to run down her arm as she shrieked with pain. Dale grabbed her and spun her around so that her back was placed against him tightly. She continued to struggle until Dale placed the tip of the blade under her chin. Then she fell still and silent. Breathing heavily and sweating with fear, she began to cry. Just then the door opened and Stephen yelled into the house, "Sweetheart, are you OK? I thought I heard you scream." Upon seeing his girlfriend in the arms of danger, he stepped forward immediately to help. Dale slowly shook his head from side to side and pressed the steel tip harder into her chin. A drop of blood ran down the shaft of his weapon. Stephen stopped, raised both hands with his palms facing Dale, and pleaded for her safety. "OK, OK, Dale, don't hurt..."

"You shut up now. I want you to find some rope. Do you have rope?" Dale interrupted him, uninterested in his pleas for mercy.

"No, we don't have any rope, Dale. What are you doing? We trusted you," Stephen pleaded.

"Well then, in that case, I suppose I will have to change the rules a bit." Dale told Anibelle to walk toward the bed. Once they were at the edge, he instructed her to lie down after he let her go. "If you try anything, sweetie, I will cut you so bad no one will ever know who you were."

She did as he requested, crying and trembling with fear. Stephen began to bargain his life for hers, which only caused a deep laugh to escape from Dale.

"You walk over to the foot of the bed and close your eyes," Dale instructed Stephen. He still chuckled with the thought of letting either of them go anywhere other than the afterlife. Dale watched as Stephen stood, still contemplating a different course of action. So he leaned over and dragged his blade across Anibelle's naked thigh. She screamed loudly as the wound opened. She instinctively bent forward, and

Dale snatched her by her long dark hair and re-issued his demand with the knife point at her neck. This time there was no thought for Stephen; he walked to the foot of the bed, looked at Anibelle, and said, "I love you, my dear. We shall be together again with no pain and no fear. Reach for God for He will provide the comfort." He blew her a kiss and closed his eyes for the last time. Anibelle began to fight again against Dale's grasp, and he realized she could be trouble so he hit the back of her head with the handle of his knife, which knocked her out.

Dale looked up at Stephen, who stood stoically with his eyes still closed. Tears ran from his eyes but he did not blubber; instead, he prayed rapidly. Dale walked over to him and asked, "Have you gotten a response yet?"

Stephen said, "Yes, Dale, I have. You will pay for the torture and heinous acts you have committed here and when you do pay your penance, think of me. Think of what I tell you now... One day there will be a soul you cannot defeat. You will be the scared one, you will be the one who is full of fear and unnerved by the fight the enemy brings you. God will see this through and He will see you burn in hell for eternity." Then Stephen fell silent and smiled as he moved his mouth through his prayer.

Dale's dream sprung into his mind and he began to shake and sweat immediately. Hatred for Stephen coursed through him at an alarming rate and he began to stab him wildly and maliciously. Stephen made only a few groans and grunts, but no screams. He held that display of pain in. He would not let Dale enjoy his kill. Dale followed Stephen's body to the floor, stabbing and stabbing. When Dale finished, he was bathed in the blood of his latest playing partner, but this had not been the game he intended. He looked up at the bed and saw Anibelle still lying peacefully. He wiped the blood across his face in an attempt to wipe it away. He looked at his hands as if they were not his own. He had lost control of his body and his mind for the first time. He stood up and spasms attacked his shoulders and back so severely he had to kneel to the floor and stretch against the cramps. Pain, pain, oh, how he hated pain.

Dale went to the kitchen and found a pitcher of water. He gulped down as much as his body could hold then spastically threw it all up. Afterward, he drank slowly until he began to feel his strength return. He had to clear his mind to finish his game. Rest could wait until tomorrow.

He walked into the bedroom with more water and slowly patted Anibelle's head. He had hit her hard and her head was bleeding from the blow. She started to move slowly, then her eyes winced from the pain she felt all over her body. When her senses returned, she remembered what had happened. She sprung up and widened her eyes. Pain shot through her head and leg. She felt someone beside her and turned sharply, causing a spasm in her stiff neck. She caught a glimpse of Dale smiling as she closed her eyes to fight off the pain she was feeling. "Welcome back, my dear. Are you ready to play now, or would you like some water first?"

She waved a hand at him and told him to do his will and move on. "I will not allow you to gain pleasure from providing me with any amount of comfort." She tried to sound strong, but the pain she felt was causing voice to falter.

Dale snorted a laugh. "Comfort is the last thing I wish to provide you. Just thought you could use some water. However, we shall continue as you requested."

She may have wished to respond to this, but Dale did not afford her the time. He finished her off with a quick jab of his knife through her voice box, then walked out of the house, down the road, and crossed the street.

Covered in Stephen's blood, he looked at Bill's door for a moment before walking in. The bell sounded.

Dale had struggled with the decision on how to send Bill to his maker. He wanted it to be quick, but he also wanted Bill to know as he was leaving this world that Dale was the one who had succeeded in winning the game. He was, after all, the one who played it best. This was his checkmate move.

Dale took his boots off, walked over to the register counter, and grabbed a couple of towels that were supposed to be packed. This would not happen. He wiped off what blood he could and thought dreamily of bathing in a couple of hot baths to get the rest of the blood off. Time to move on, as Anibelle put it.

He walked upstairs and found Bill still sleeping peacefully and comfortably in his bed. He walked over to the bed and stood there examining his next competitor. He stepped to the side of Bill's bed and knelt down by his head. "Bill, wake up, buddy, I need to tell you something," he said as he lightly shook him. "Come on, man, wake up. It is important."

"What is it, Dale? What's happened?" Bill questioned, still groggy from his dreams.

"I want you to lie still and hear what I have to say before you get all upset." Dale paused long enough to steady himself and make sure Bill was listening. "I am the reaper. I am the piper. I am the player of games. I have brought death to your town and you, my friend, and I do mean that. You are my last game. I shall make it quick and as painless as I can. You have helped me and I shall repay that kindness with my own." Dale calmly spoke, with a sincere smile of gratitude and mercy.

"What? What are you saying, Dale?" Bill said as he rose quickly on his elbows.

He would have asked more, but Dale held true to his words and brought his hand across Bill's chest with the knife blade pointing back at Dale. He pulled back toward his body, slicing into Bill's neck to the hilt of the handle. He then stood back from the bed and watched as Bill pulled the knife out and dropped it on the bed, as he left his body behind and let his spirit slip into the light.

Dale made it back to his house, completely drained from the day's events. He went to the bedroom immediately and slept without even taking his clothes off.

Dale woke in the morning and took his long awaited baths. Then he gorged himself on food and went back to bed, sleeping until the next day. Dale then settled in for the remainder of the winter. He needed to charge his batteries and with the troops of the South threatening to move north, he didn't want to be caught in the middle of a battle somewhere, trying to move on to another playing ground.

***

Once spring arrived, Dale headed into town and began his job of lighting each structure on fire. Everyone who he didn't get to play games with had left town with no intentions of returning, but eventually someone would come for whatever reason, and he didn't want people asking questions about the bodies that were found. He could shift the blame away from him when it came to a mass fire, but dead bodies, not really. Stevenson was gone and would never come back.

Over the next couple of months, Dale worked in the garden and began to prepare wood for the next winter. He wouldn't be needing it, but how would he know that?

As summer began, Dale felt the desire to start another round of games. Hagerstown would be the next game board.

He started going to Hagerstown a couple times a week and made sure to speak to Judge Remmy at least once a week. In early July, he stumbled across his first player, a young boy out fishing at a nearby creek. Dale walked up to him and asked how his luck was going. The young man turned and smiled and said things were going pretty good. He showed Dale his line and there were four nice trout strung out. Dale talked to him for a while then asked if his parents were around. The boy slyly smiled and said, "Nope. I'm supposed to be at home doing chores, but I figured I had some time to get some fishin' in." The boy laughed as he raised his finger to his mouth in a shushing motion.

Dale chuckled. "Mums the word, buddy. Well, you have a good day, son, and good luck with the fish," he said as he walked behind him. Dale grabbed the young man, who had just enough time to give a shout of disapproval, before his head was submerged in the water. The kicking and fighting didn't last long and when the young man, who would never get older, fell still, Dale pushed the rest of him in the water. Dale dried off his hands on his pants, grabbed the trout string, and went home to feast on the fresh catch.

On Dale's next trip to Hagerstown, he spoke to the judge about the impending Southern invasion. The judge said there were some families that were leaving until things cooled down some. Dale smiled and offered up his home as a safe house, so to speak. The judge laughed and said, "Son, you must have been sent straight from heaven." However,

Dale was sent from a place much farther south than even the troops who were on their way.

***

Dale didn't end up becoming a safe house for the families of Hagerstown; he ended up becoming a death trap. Over the course of a few weeks, families showed up, and before the next family could arrive, Dale would kill them one by one, disposing of the bodies in one fashion or another. He buried the first family but began to resent the work involved. So he began to store them in the barn, where he covered them with lye. Some he took out into the woods and let nature's animals feast on the corpses. One way or the other, they all died. Horrors that couldn't be real were brought down on trusting souls.

It was now late August, and Dale was sleeping soundly after playing another successful round of games with the latest family to come looking for help. He was awakened by shouting in his house. As he went to sit up in bed, four men entered his room and stopped quickly, terror and anger in their eyes. They began shouting at him to get up, get up now. Dale sat still, smiling, knowing his game was over, but he had played it well and he had played it for a long time.

The Southern soldiers afforded him no courtesies and beat him with each story he told of his days in Stevenson. However, this didn't seem to faze Dale. He enjoyed the reaction he was getting. As he answered questions and took his beatings, other soldiers were removing the bodies of the innocent victims left in his wake of recent destruction. He would look briefly at the bodies until he was hit, forcing him to look back at the officer asking the questions.

The commanding officer asked Dale to write a confession and Dale agreed.

I DID IT. I DID IT ALL. I PLAYED MY GAMES AND WON. AND I WILL PLAY THEM AGAIN. YOU CAN'T STOP EVIL, YOU CAN'T STOP THE DEVIL, YOU ARE NOT THAT STRONG.

> DALE PLUSH
> THE GAME MASTER

Dale was taken outside and he scanned the area to see the faces of disbelief. As he looked from soldier to soldier, his eye caught a glimpse of an old friend. Jet black hair, solid white legs from the knee down, and a white stripe on her left ear. Nell stood stoically, seeing the man who had left her to her own devices. Dale paused to take in the enjoyment of seeing her alive until he was pushed forward by the guard trailing him. A hood was placed over his head after he climbed up onto Storm's broad back. While he sat there on Storm, in the blackness, with his hands tied tightly behind his back, he saw that little boy from his dream and fear filled him. The presence of another was strong just as it was in his dream and then he heard something. Was it a growl, a very low growl? Then a burly bark snapped him straight, just as the rope pulled tight and snapped his neck.v

AWARENESS

MARY WAS APPALLED by what she was reading. Fortunately for her, the article didn't have many details of what took place. She did, however, read enough to make her sick to her stomach. She didn't even know someone could have enough evil in them to do such things. The worst part of it was she had moved her family into the home of one of the worst serial killers in U.S. history. What was she to do now? She had to tell Donnie. But what about Robbie's dreams and the things he had told her that were happening to him? Could it be the spirit of Dale haunting her home? *Oh, God, what's happening to them?* she thought.

Mary went home and talked to Donnie that night while the kids were in bed. She told him everything she had read and that she was scared that maybe everything Robbie was telling them wasn't just his imagination. Donnie answered calmly and logically, "Mary, if that's what's happening, then why is he the only one affected by this guy's spirit? I agree it is tragic what took place, but you know I don't believe in evil spirits and demons."

Bandit knew what Mary was saying was right. Robbie knew what he was seeing was real. Mary knew they had to leave. Donnie knew he wasn't moving.

***

Dale sensed a changed in the house. Even in his current capacity, he could still feel the mood changes. He felt more power than he had ever felt since hanging in that damn tree. Fear. Fear fed him. Fear made him stronger. He was sure that the boy he had dreamt of while still walking the earth was Robbie, and the force he had sensed in that dream was that blasted dog, but now the fear level in the house was rising and making him more and more capable of playing his games.

Mary moved around the house with caution, looking for things to happen. She stayed in constant anticipation but eventually her nerves began to relax. She didn't want to believe, she really didn't. But she did and the thought of that man haunting her baby filled her with terror.

This was of course the fear that was feeding Dale his power.

Robbie began to experience small episodes of strangeness again. The steps in the hall sounded louder than before, the door seemed to spring open and closed again, and the figure began to speak to him again. Last night the voice was firm and bold as it was before, but still Robbie did not react as he did before. In fact, when Bandit first began to growl at the hallway, Robbie smiled at him and said, "Let's play a game, Bandit. The man wants to play, then let's play." Then he laughed and Bandit pulled his lips back, which resembled a grin.

The steps got closer to the door, and Robbie stepped on the floor and put his hand on Bandit's head. The door opened and the figure stepped into view. Robbie noticed he seemed to be a bit more real tonight. More color than before and more profound, but he still wasn't scary. "What is your name?" he asked the man.

The Game Evil Plays

"My name is Dale Plush, child. Are you ready to play my games yet, boy?" Dale inquired with a smile.

"Well, Dale, my name is Robbie and I don't want to play your game, but maybe you would like to play *our* games," Robbie teased. Bandit took a step toward the man speaking at the door.

Dale looked at the dog and the boy for a moment then spoke in a fevered yell, "You do not know who you are messing with, young one!"

At that, Bandit stepped in front of Robbie and stood proudly to defend his friend. Robbie took a step forward and spoke lightly to Dale. "I think you do not know who you are messing with, *sir*." He pointed to Bandit with a knowing grin.

"Not everyone in this house can be watched by your dog at the same time. I will start with whomever I have to to get you, boy. Our game begins now." Dale moved toward the two opponents, but they held their ground. At the same time they both leapt at Dale, Bandit with sharpened teeth and Robbie with hardened fists. Then Dale was gone. Gone, till next time.

That night, Robbie dreamt of people he didn't know, but they all seemed so nice to him. John was the man he liked the most. He used to live in this house with his wife, Elizabeth, and his pretty daughter, Becca. They smiled and sang songs by their fireplace and just when Robbie was about to leave dreamland, John walked over to Robbie and told him that if he ever needed help there was a bunch of folks ready to beat Dale at his game. All Robbie had to do was think of them and they would be right by his side.

Robbie woke and told his mother of his wonderful dream and his new friends. Mary quickly responded, "Baby, sometimes people seem nice, but they're not nice at all. Sometimes people are mean and they want to hurt people. Please be careful, baby." She had tears in her eyes.

Robbie looked at his mother, confused. "Mommy, I know Dale is mean. Bandit and I don't like him very much, but we aren't scared of him anymore. Well, Bandit never was," he said with boyish charm. "John and his family are nice though. I know it just the same way I know Dale is mean. I can feel it, Mommy. I will be OK, I promise. I will protect you all from Dale until we can beat him at his game." Robbie winked and kissed her on her cheek.

***

For the next several weeks, Robbie and Bandit had standoffs with Dale and each ended the same way. So when Dale showed up tonight, Robbie played like he couldn't hear Dale talking to him and just avoided him altogether. Then Dale's hatred grew to a whole new level and he shouted, "If you can't hear me then you won't be able to hear this. I am going to kill your mother!"

With that, Robbie shot up and replied, "Bandit and John won't let that happen, but if you say you are going to do that again, then I will call all of John's friends to help beat you now and win the game for good." Robbie couldn't remember ever being so angry in his whole life.

Dale looked at Robbie with amazement and just a bit of confusion and apprehension. How could he possibly know John and, how did he put it, his friends? That couldn't mean everyone from town...could it? Could they even help him if they tried? He hadn't heard from any of them since taking them out of this world. Had they been waiting for this boy and his dog this whole time?

"You better be careful with who you choose as partners in this game, kid. Everyone you speak of has already lost their own game with me. I doubt they would serve you any better," he said with uncertainty in his voice. It was strong enough for a child to read.

"Well, then, you shouldn't be scared, should you? Just don't think I won't do whatever it takes to protect my family." Robbie narrowed his eyes at Dale the exact moment Bandit did, and they launched an attack on the apparition simultaneously and he vanished. They had won again. This time.

That night Robbie dreamt of a guy reading a book by a cozy fire, like his mommy liked to do. Robbie walked into the room and sat on the floor, looking up at the man behind his book. The man moved the book and smiled at Robbie. He said, "I heard from a friend of mine that you're having some troubles, young man. You may have an extra headache to worry with, I'm afraid. My daughter may cause you some issues. Her name is Sarah and she helped Dale long ago, so he may turn to her for help again. Tell her when you see her that her daddy loves her. Will you do that for me, son? In return, I will help you if I can. Just call for me. My name is Benjamin, but Ben will work for our agreement." Benjamin paused and a tear slid down his face. "Now you get on back to sleep, sonny. You will need your energy, and I would like to get back to my reading. Good luck to you, young man." Benjamin raised the book again and began to read.

Bandit woke Robbie from his dream by licking his face. "Do you ever sleep, boy?" Robbie asked, then realized the sun was shining brightly into his room. "OK, boy, OK, let's go," Robbie said as he crawled out of bed.

Robbie loved summertime. He liked school, but he sure loved the summer. He got to run around outside all day and play with Bandit. He slept in the yard under the sun. He went fishing, rode his bike, and spent time with his mom. Smiling, he went to his mom and asked how she was. He had kept the last dream to himself, because he knew what Ben said would have scared her. "Well, I'm OK, sweetie. How have you been? I worry for you and the dreams you have. I worry you may be in trouble. I love you, Robbie, and if anything were to ever happen to you, I don't know what I would do," she proclaimed.

"Mommy, I love you too." He walked to her and hugged her. "Don't be afraid, Mommy. Bandit and I are not afraid of the bad man and we will win the game. I promise." Robbie smiled and went back out to Bandit.

"Can you read my mind, buddy? Can you see my dreams when I sleep? Do you know about Sarah and the good man, Ben?" Robbie asked Bandit as he looked into his friend's coal black eyes. Bandit leaned forward and licked Robbie's forehead then nudged him with his nose on the same spot. "OK, so you can. Good. I may need you to help me call on our friends if something happens to me. Nothing can happen to Mom, Bandit. I love her as much as I love you. I love the whole family, but that's my mommy and Dale can't have her." He hugged Bandit. "Together we will win. Together somehow we will defeat him."

Robbie and Bandit went to the creek, down the road from their house, and sat on the bank, fishing and playing in the water. After a couple hours, Robbie decided to head home. As they approached the house, he could see two shapes moving upstairs in the windows. Bandit sensed the beings as well. They walked in the house and the two of them, side by side, started up the stairs when a girl's voice sounded out at them. "Come on up here, little boy. Bring your body guard along. We have a lot to do to get ready for the game."

Once they reached the top, Robbie leaned to the side and told Bandit to be steady. Then the door to his room opened and there stood an older girl dressed in old pants and a worn out jacket. *This must be Sarah*, he thought. She was still pretty but pain was evident. Pain seemed to move her. She moved toward the two friends, then Robbie spoke. "I talked to your daddy, Sarah. He wants me to tell you that he still loves you."

Sarah stopped and replied, "My daddy is dead. He can't talk to you, boy. I killed him."

"I saw him in my dream. He was reading a book by the fire and asked me to tell you that."

Sarah paused with that response. Could this boy really have spoken to her father? If not, then how did he know her dad sat by the fire reading a book? Dale said this boy could be a tricky player, but he was just a boy after all. *Then why does Dale need me? Why did he call upon me to aid him, to be partners in this game?*

Robbie saw confusion on her face. She looked like she was trying to solve one of those hard math riddles he hated so much. "Sarah, your daddy still loves you even if you did kill him. He told me that. Dale is playing a game with you and you had better be careful with him. He is a bad man. He is evil and mean and only likes to scare and hurt people. We're not scared of him so he is using you to help him, but what happens to you when he doesn't need you anymore?"

Sarah flashed back to that night at Dale's after she had disposed of her father's life. When all was supposed to be perfect, Dale turned on her and killed her.

Suddenly from behind Sarah, Dale appeared, and he was fuming with anger. Robbie had never gotten a good look at him because it was always dark and the shadows hid him for the most part. He wished he hadn't seen him now. His neck was long and skinny and his head seemed too big to stay up right, but it did. His eyes were big and dark and his teeth looked like those of a shark Robbie had seen on TV. His cheeks were so sunken in they seemed to touch each other. His hair was wild and mangy. Evil had eaten away at him for years, it appeared.

"Shut your mouth, boy!" he snarled. "You do not know the things you speak of. Do not attempt to complicate the matter with lies!"

Robbie froze for just a second and then Dale grinned. Dale knew his appearance and his tone had scared the boy, and this he liked very much.

Bandit, however, had seen Dale the first night and had not cared of his looks. It was his spirit he hated and nothing had changed since then. He took a step forward and growled, then snapped his own razor-sharp teeth at Dale.

"I have had enough of you, fur ball!" Dale shouted from the pit of his black soul. He moved past Sarah and came within a few feet of Bandit. Robbie unfroze and saw his friend in trouble. Bandit was standing firm and showed no signs of weakness, but Dale seemed too strong right now.

Robbie stepped beside Bandit and did the only thing that came to his mind. He brought up his hands and formed a cross with his two index fingers and said loudly, bravely, and proudly, "Go away, Dale! Leave my friend alone. I love him and I won't let you hurt him!"

It was Dale's turn to freeze.

THE FIRST MOVE

A N EIGHT-YEAR-OLD DALE looked at his dad, pleading with him to not do it. "Please, Daddy, don't! I love her so much! I will fix her, I will fix her, Daddy, I promise!"

Jacob Plush was a farmer in Tennessee and like most farmers he had a "heart for God and a mind for sod," or so was his little joke. He loved God, his family, and farming, in that order. So when poor Dale's young mare, Summer, came down with a fever he knew what had to be done. Even as his son begged and begged for him to please stop, Jacob pulled the trigger and shot Summer in the head. Jacob cried for his son's loss and did not take it personally when Dale screamed, "I hate you!"

Dale refused to eat that night, he refused to do his chores, and he refused to come out of his room. He was so hurt and mad, mostly hurt, by his loss. But the madness was there, peeking for an opportunity to come out. Dale's mother, Catherine, cried when Jacob told her the tale and tried to go to her son, but Dale refused her loved. She sat down on the floor outside of his room, trying to explain that what his daddy did was necessary. "As hard as it is to do that, it was the best thing for Summer, sweetie, I promise. She was in so much pain. She wasn't going to get better. Better to put her down than to let her suffer."

"She was my friend, she was my friend! *I LOVED HER!*" Dale yelled back at her.

That night Dale prayed for Summer to come back. He prayed the next night and the next and for the next week or so. Each night, though, his passion behind his words lessened and his faith weakened. How could God allow this to happen? The devil made Summer sick, so God could have made her better, right? Then that question changed to Maybe God isn't so strong, maybe the devil is stronger. Maybe that is why *He* cast the devil to hell, because *He* knew he was more powerful. "I want to have that kind of power, and then no one I love will ever have to die again." This prayer would be his last.

That night, while dreaming, Dale was visited by the unholy. His wish had been heard and he was about to receive what he wanted, though he didn't truly want it. But evil doesn't allow us to think twice. Once you open your mind and heart to a thought like that, evil slides in, devouring the good, elevating the hate, and eliminating emotion and logic. What's left is a body wrapped around darkness and controlled by Hell.

Dale woke just before dawn and burned his house to the ground. He started the fire in his baby sister's room. Then he went in to his parents' room, lit the curtain by the window, then walked to the doorway and started another fire. As the fires grew, he tossed his lantern on the bed and watched his parents burn as they screamed and pleaded for relief. He then ran outside, where he collapsed.

Dale spent the next eight or so years in and out of different homes. The last of these homes was that of Gerald and Judy Starcrest. They had never had any kids of their own, but both loved helping young people. They lived in the Smokey Mountains and had five children living with them already before the pastor told them about Dale. They went to see Dale and liked him right away. He was very friendly and polite. Dale began living with them two months later. Two months after that, the bodies of Gerald, Judy, and the five children were discovered by the pastor after the family had missed two weeks of services. Dale was gone. He had already started walking. He didn't stop walking until he reached the little town of Stevenson.

THE GAME

"CHILD, YOU WILL not always be able to save your friends. This is a lesson you should learn sooner rather than later. I can give you the power to never lose anyone you love. I can make you never feel pain. I can do all this for your friend there as well. If you let me." Dale spoke to Robbie with the emotion he had forgotten but also with the evil he now knew.

"I do not want to be like you. You hurt people and scare people. You scared me and you liked it. Bandit never felt that fear and you hate him for it. I don't fear you and we will win your game. Now leave us alone," Robbie said to Dale. His voice was stronger than he ever heard himself sound. He felt stronger inside. He felt vibrant.

Dale stepped back again then stood slightly behind Sarah, who had been watching silently. She stared at Bandit and spoke with her mind. *Small soldier, but powerful. I feel your love, but it is too late for me. Protect your keeper. He is strong but not strong enough. Never leave him. Dale is too preoccupied with him to sense this, so listen quickly. Love and kindness... Pure of heart, these are the things that can hurt him, but I do not know how to beat him. Good luck to you both. Tell my daddy I'm sorry for who I became and what I did.*

Unfortunately, Dale was not too preoccupied to hear the end of her thoughts. He looked at her with disgust, reached into her back, stole her essence, and swallowed it whole. Robbie stood and watched as Sarah faded. She cried as she went back to the pits of hell for eternity.

Dale began to convulse as Sarah's darkness spread through him. Robbie thought to Bandit, *Now,* and they both sprang forward into Dale's aura, forcing him to retreat into the house.

Robbie lay on the floor exhausted, catching his breath, when he heard footsteps on the stairs. Bandit snapped around and began to growl again and Robbie sighed. He didn't know if he could play another game so quickly. Then Bandit stopped growling and licked his face.

"Robbie, sweetie, are you OK?" his mother asked, crying.

"Mom, I'm fine, we're fine." *Did she hear everything?* He hoped not. He got up and walked to the top of the stairs. "Sorry, Mom, we were playing and I fell."

"Honey, I felt fear for you. I heard a girl tell me to help you. Baby, please come down here. We need to talk."

The boy looked at his friend and thought, *Come on, boy. Mom wants to talk to us.* The two walked side by side down the stairs.

The three of them sat outside as Matt played in the yard and Leslie slept on a blanket in front of them. "Are we in danger, Robbie?" she asked.

"I don't think so. Dale, the bad man, wants to play a game with me. A bad game, I know that. Bandit isn't afraid of him and the two of us together can beat him. He gets scared when we're together and stand against him." Robbie didn't want to lie to his mom, but he wanted to make her feel safe, and more importantly, unafraid. Fear was a powerful food for Dale.

"I don't want you to do this, baby. I want you to stop playing with him and he will go away. Just ignore him. I will get us out of here soon."

"Mom, I can't stop because he won't stop. If we move, the next family will be here for him to play with and they won't have Bandit. *He* is the strong one. I just follow him and do what feels right," Robbie said.

"I'm going to tell your daddy. He can help you. Help you both, I mean," Mary replied. She tried to think of a logical answer but couldn't.

"Mom, Dad doesn't believe, which is good. I think Matt is too young to see the evil and Leslie is too young too. I don't like that you know, because Dale could come after you. Never let him feel your fear. Trust in your heart, Mom. Trust in good. Trust in us, but most importantly, trust in God. I think I will have to call on our friends next time. I'm really tired after this last game. Bandit can go and go, but it makes me tired. I don't know how to win yet, though, and I worry about that. I think Bandit will figure it out and tell me."

"You can talk to him? Bandit talks to you, baby?" Mary was amazed.

"Not like us, Mom." Robbie giggled a little bit. "We can hear each other in our heads. He can hear me more than I can hear him, but it works for us. Watch." Robbie looked at Bandit and asked him with his thoughts first then said out loud, "Look at Mom, buddy, and smile!" Bandit looked at Robbie, tilted his head, then looked over at Mary and pulled his lips back. Then he dropped his head back to the ground.

Mary gasped, "Oh, my good Lord."

Robbie laughed and rubbed Bandit's head. "He wasn't sure what I meant by *smile*."

Mary wasn't sure what to say and the conversation flattened out. Robbie said he was tired and needed a nap. So he lay on his back, with his head on Bandit's side, and the two warriors closed their eyes and slept.

***

"Hello there, young man, my name is Stephen and this is Anibelle. It is a pleasure to meet you, and you as well, Bandit. We're here to help you. I knew God would send us the answer and He has not disappointed."

Robbie looked down and saw Bandit by his side. Bandit hadn't joined him in a dream before. This was cool. "Hello, my name is Robbie and this is my best friend Bandit, but you already know that I guess. I don't know if we are the answers. I don't know how to win. I don't know how to beat Dale at his game."

Stephen and Anibelle looked at one another and smiled. "Your friend there does, Robbie. He told us goodness, love, and pure hearts will defeat him. And we can tell you both have those qualities. You have to find a way to harness the power of God's gifts and use that against him. When the time comes, you call on us and we will provide you the strength to fight. Now rest, Robbie, rest well. The time is nearing for you to play the end game. We are all with you. Godspeed." Then Robbie and Bandit woke, the sun still warming their bodies.

The two friends walked around the yard and ended up on the backside of the house, in the far left corner, where the wildflowers bloomed. Robbie stopped just outside the area of the flowers. Bandit paused and then stepped into the center. *Come,* he said to Robbie. Robbie seemed amused then stepped into the flower patch with his buddy. Then a slow tingling feeling began to touch Robbie's skin until he shivered. He smiled and giggled. Bandit seemed to shake as if he needed to get water off his fur. Robbie was happy and love ran through his veins. He smiled and allowed the feeling to overtake him. Bandit stopped shaking and stood still, soaking in the love. Robbie looked down at Bandit and did not see his dog. He saw the spirit of an angel. The feeling weakened then stopped. Robbie looked back to Bandit and his buddy was standing there, looking up at him, tongue out and panting. Robbie felt fully restored. His nap had helped. He now not only felt physically stronger but mentally as well.

Bandit led his companion into the house. Robbie played with Matt while Bandit lay sleeping just a few feet away, but keeping his senses running at peak performance. When Donnie came home, the family sat and ate a wonderful meal, then Robbie helped his mom clean the table and dishes. Afterward, he went outside with Bandit, before bed, to walk around and look at the stars while Bandit did his business. He stood on the sidewalk and looked up into the night and the lights above him. He wondered all the wonders a boy has when looking at space. Bandit came to him and nudged his leg then walked to the door.

Robbie walked upstairs behind Bandit, with no signs of Dale. He knelt beside his bed and prayed for his family to be safe, for God to watch over Bandit, and to help him think of how he was supposed to beat Dale. Then he slid into bed and drifted off to sleep while Bandit lay at his feet, looking at the door until the Sandman called his name.

***

Robbie stood in front of a door. There was nothing on either side of it. He reached for the doorknob, pushed it open, and stepped inside as a bell sounded his entrance.

Robbie looked around the store and liked the cozy feeling. He walked between the racks of shirts and the counters with boxes of buttons and rolls of fabric that his mommy would love. "Hello there, young fella," a man's voice sounded. Robbie turned and saw a man standing behind the counter with a big smile on his face. "Nice to finally get to meet you. My name is Bill. I believe you would be Robbie. I was hoping to get to meet your friend, Bandit. Best friend I would guess."

"Yes sir, he is my best friend. I love him very much," Robbie confirmed.

Smiling and nodding, Bill replied, "Yes son, I know that. It's as plain to see as the nose on your face." Now his smile faded. "I had me a best friend once. Turned out to be the devil incarnate. I never had that kind of bond, and when I thought I had, I learned too late that I was being manipulated." Bill sighed and relived that horrible moment in his mind. It wasn't the blade in his neck that hurt the most; it was the feeling of betrayal that destroyed him. "Son, I'm sure by now you know that Dale is not just an evil person or being, he *is* evil. He is the thing that scares us the most, he is the nightmare that won't go away, he is the demon of hell. He will do whatever it takes to win, and you have to be ready. You have to be strong. Your heart will be tested, your soul will be tormented, but you must stand solid."

"Bill, we will be strong, Bandit and I together will be rocks. I will not let Dale play his games with anyone else ever again. I promise," Robbie said.

"Well, now, I believe that. Keep your mind clear, son, so when you need us you can call on us. Be safe and stay close to your friend. We are all counting for you." Then Bill was gone.

Robbie woke to his mom yelling and crying. He jumped up out of bed and went to his door, where Bandit had already been, checking things out. He walked into the hallway and saw his mom leaning over Matt's bed. Donnie was standing on the other side of the bed, trying to calm her and Matt down. Then Robbie saw the blood all over the top of Matt's bed. "What's going on? Is Matt OK?"

"Robbie, he will be fine. He woke with a bloody nose. Why don't you go down to the kitchen and get us a wet tea towel, please," Donnie said.

Robbie turned quickly and ran down the stairs and into the kitchen. He opened the towel drawer, snatched a towel, and then soaked it under the faucet, wringing it out good. He started across the dining room when he heard Dale laughing. He spun around but Dale wasn't there. The laugh remained and it got stronger and stronger. "Dale, I warned you about touching my family. I will beat you if you dare to face me. Leave everyone out of this. This is between us," Robbie boldly said as he started toward the stairs again.

"You little boy, with your stupid dog. I look forward to playing my game and watching fear eat you alive. I look forward to taking your souls and torturing them daily for eternity." Dale laughed.

"You're scared of us. I know it and you know it. You will pay for what you did to Matt." Robbie reached the top of the stairs, where Bandit was looking at him, wondering why he had left without him. Robbie patted his head and walked down the hall to Matt's room. He handed the towel to Donnie and shared a knowing glance with his mother. Robbie and Bandit went into their room, where they sat on the floor, talking without words about what needed to be done.

Mary walked in the room and caught a glimpse of this meeting and started to cry again. She could tell the end game had begun. Hurting Matt was the first move to push Robbie into the fight. "Robbie, this game of yours has gone on long enough. We're leaving."

Robbie and Bandit slowly looked at Mary and the look in their eyes and the expression on their faces caused her to step back. She had never seen Robbie look so serious and mature. Not to mention the fact that the two of them turned their heads at the same time, with the same expression, as if they were mirror images of each other.

"Mom, you are correct. The game has gone on long enough and it needs to stop. You all should leave now. Don't come back till tomorrow. I don't know how long it will take to finish the game and we don't want anyone coming in and getting hurt. Go tell Dad you want to stay at Grandma's tonight and that Bandit and I want to go to John's house down the road. I'm sorry for what happened to Matt, but it will never happen again. If, when you come back tomorrow and we are not waiting for you outside, do not come in. Just leave," Robbie instructed his mother.

Mary stood blinking. She could not believing the uneasy calmness coming from her son, but what she felt next took her over the top. *Leave, now, please... I love you. I will protect him for you.* She looked into Bandit's cool black eyes and he nodded at her.

She could say nothing. She couldn't move. She was having trouble breathing normally. Bandit barked loudly and snapped her out of her trance-like state. She looked at Robbie as tears rolled down her cheeks. She walked over to him, knelt, and kissed him on the forehead. Then she kissed Bandit on his head and Bandit returned a lick to her cheek.

Mary convinced Donnie to stay at Henry and Marie's house. Robbie was right, though. He didn't even flinch when she said Robbie and Bandit were staying at the house. Robbie and Bandit walked them all out to the car. He kissed his little sister and brother goodbye. Then he listened as his dad issued rules for their night alone. Fortunately, Donnie never said Robbie couldn't fight the devil and his demon soul.

Robbie hugged his mother tightly. She looked at him closely and he whispered into her ear, "I know you will want to come back but don't. Your fear of us getting hurt may give Dale too much extra power. I know you love me and would do anything for me, but today I need you to stay away. This is *my* time to protect *you*. It is my turn to rock you, Mommy, and make you feel safe and loved... I love you very much. Don't worry. Goodbye." Then he walked away and turned back to the car as they started to drive away. He threw up his hand in a good-natured wave then bent down to Bandit. "Let's do this, buddy. Let's go win the end game."

Bandit replied with two quick, deep barks and the two friends walked side by side back into the house, where the game would be played to the death.

THE END GAME

❦

BANDIT LOOKED AROUND sensing Dale but not strongly, not yet. That time was soon approaching. Robbie and Bandit slowly walked up the steps. No need to rush. The game would be played tonight for sure. They walked into their room and sat as they were earlier, in the middle of the floor facing each other. Robbie ran the names through his mind into Bandit's: *John, Ben, Stephen, Anibelle, and Bill. John, Ben, Stephen, Anibelle, and Bill.* Bandit suggested a walk out to the flower patch to rejuvenate their minds and souls, and Robbie agreed.

The two stood and the door slammed shut. There would be no walk to the patch. Dale laughed and threw the door open, which sent a cold wind through the room. The door slammed shut again then sprung open, and a wave of bats flew into the room. They swirled around and dived toward Robbie and Bandit, swerving at the last minute as Robbie swung his hands to deflect the expected impact. As one of the bats flew closely to Bandit, he lunged forward and snapped his powerful jaws, instantly crushing the bat. The other bats stopped their flight and disappeared, including the bat in Bandit's mouth. Bandit pulled his lips back and growled at the door, and Robbie waited.

Nothing happened for a few minutes, then the door exploded and shattered into a thousand pieces. It happened so fast that Robbie had no time to defend himself. The only thing he could do was put his hands up to protect his face, but one piece sliced the right side of his cheek. He touched his cheek and saw the blood on his hand. "Is that all you got, Dale? Step into the room and face us!" Bandit barked to add the exclamation to Robbie's words.

"You can't win, child. I will kill you and your mutt, and I will savor the taste of your soul." Dale spoke with an ease and confidence only the arrogant possess.

Robbie laughed this time. "Were you scary when you were alive? If you were, you've lost it since then. Now, come to us and take your loss."

Dale roared and the house shook.

Bandit growled back and Robbie yelled to show no fear.

Dale stepped into the doorway and pointed at his two opponents. "You dare mock me and my power? You think you can defeat me by angering me? I have killed more people than you have ever known, and you stand before me, small and insignificant, threatening me with words? I shall take my time destroying you!"

Robbie stepped forward and forcefully replied, "I mock you because you do nothing but slam doors and hurt people when they sleep. You will pay for all the people you have killed, and I stand before you large with the power of love and kindness. I will show you mercy if you ask for forgiveness for the things you have done and take your punishment in hell for eternity."

A fire enveloped Dale and swirled around him. He raised his hands and threw a heated energy toward Robbie. Robbie placed his hands up in front of him, not to block the energy, but to catch it. When it hit his hands, he felt the evil trying to eat into his skin. The heat was intense, but fading quickly.

Robbie tossed his hand to the right and discarded the waste of the assault onto the floor.

The fire around Dale intensified and as he started to build another dagger of heat, Robbie stepped closer with Bandit and pulled out a cross. It was from one of his mom's necklaces. She had given it to him as they stood by the car. At the sight of the cross, Dale hollered in agony and the fire was extinguished.

A look of surprise flashed across Dale's face, and he reached out and grabbed Robbie by the shirt in a desperate attempt. Bandit wasn't having any of it. He jumped up and bit into Dale's illusion of an arm, causing him to let go of Robbie because the hand lost its power due to the power of the bite.

Robbie stepped back and asked honestly, "Why do you hate so much, Dale? Why do you have to hurt people? It is better to love and enjoy people. Have you never loved anyone? Have you always been evil?"

"Shut your mouth, boy! I have nothing to share with you but your own misery!" Dale exclaimed with anger.

But there was a thought; a brief escape for Dale to better days before Summer was put down by his father. It was a time of happiness and love. A time when his family was the most important thing, and the thing he cherished most.

Robbie started, "Dale, I don't want to play against you, but I will if you make me. We both will, but there is a better way."

Who is this kid to play mind games with me? Who does he think he is? Dale thought to himself. He pulled his lips back and smiled, showing off his sharp, erratic teeth. "You're right, there is a better way. You both can submit to me now and enjoy my games forever." With that, he offered his hand to Robbie.

"OK, then, I guess the game is on," Robbie said rather glumly. He had hoped Dale would just change his mind, but he figured Dale wouldn't. Robbie wasn't afraid and would have rather avoided this, but he was ready either way.

"As you wish." Dale disappeared into the house. Robbie spun to look behind him then spun again to face where the door once guarded the entrance into his room. Bandit threw his nose to the air and then to the floor, sucking in any scent he could. He reached out trying to pick up a sense of Dale, but found nothing.

Robbie waited. He waited for Dale to do something, to show himself, to continue the game. But there was no sign of him; Bandit even seemed to have lost him. "Come on, boy, let's go downstairs." As he started for the stairs the glass in his bedroom window shattered. Then the window at the end of the hallway blew inward across the floor. Suddenly, there was a massive explosion of glass as every window in the house erupted with such force that Robbie lost his balance and fell to the floor.

Dale laughed at him loudly. As Dale laughed, the glass pieces in the room began to shiver and lift off the floor. Robbie looked at the glass and then to Bandit. "Help, Ben! Help, please!" Robbie requested.

"You shall die now, boy," Dale said. He was feeling cocky now. The smile which cracked his face had never been bigger. "You too, dog." He glared at Bandit. Dale raised his arms up in front of him, with his palms to the ceiling, until his hands were shoulder high. Then he rotated his hands so that his palms faced each other. "You didn't make a very good opponent after all, boy." He showed off that God-awful grin.

Ben. Please. Now. I need you, please, Robbie thought.

Dale pulled his hands a bit farther apart, and the flying glass moved a couple inches away from the pair of friends. Dale winked at Robbie and slammed his hands together so fast and hard that the smack sent a quiver through Robbie's heart. He closed his eyes and prepared for the impact of a thousand razor blades, but that did not happen. Instead, Dale roared again and Ben stood in front of the friends, with his hands raised to chest level. They rotated up, his palms facing the walls. Ben stood tall with his head held high, shoulders back, and chest out. "You took my daughter from me, Dale. She was a good girl who never meant ill will to anyone, and you turned her over to your evil ways. Your days of playing games are over. In the end, I still love my Sarah and I know she loves me, and I also know she has remorse for the things she's done. I should have killed you long, long ago, but I was too weak to do what needed to be done. Now I shall help destroy you, even if I cannot do it by myself." Ben threw his hands forward, causing the glass shards to hurl toward Dale.

The only course of action for Dale was to disappear into the floor. "Leave this house, Ben. Leave it now. You have no business here. You had your chance years ago and you lost," Dale yelled at Ben as if he was cheated.

Ben ignored this and turned to Robbie. "Are you OK, son? Did any of the glass cut you?"

"None of it hit me. Thank you for coming. Should I call everyone else too?" Robbie asked.

"I don't think so. We lose our strength the more active we are. You will need to choose carefully when you call upon us. The good news is that Dale will lose his strength too, which is why he is gone now. He is probably off absorbing energy from somewhere. You should do so yourself. Prepare

The Game Evil Plays

for the next round of the fight. I will go now too, but I will be ready if you need me again. Good luck, son." Ben faded as he walked down the hallway.

Bandit looked to Robbie and said, *Come, we must prepare.* Then he walked to the doorway and waited for Robbie. The two walked down the hallway, down the stairs, and outside to breathe in the night air. Robbie walked over to the water spigot and turned the valve wheel until water flowed in a good rush. He took some water and rubbed his face and head and the back of his neck. He cupped his hands and caught some water and drank heartily for several minutes. Then Bandit lapped at the water too. When he finished, Robbie turned the water off and nodded to Bandit, answering his question. "Yes, I do think we could use a flower patch break."

They reached the backside of the house as the sun began to set. Robbie stopped to take in the view. A beautiful orange-red sun cast an amazing display of light across the sky. Clouds moved lazily and a cool night breeze had already started to chip away at the heat. On any other day, this would be a perfect night. Tonight, of course, was far from perfect. But one must make the best of each situation so they can grow. That's what his mother said, anyway. How he loved her.

Bandit nudged his leg and they continued their walk to where the wildflowers grew. This time, neither of the two stopped. They walked directly into the center and felt the tingle as soon as they stilled their feet. Robbie closed his eyes this time and lights danced inside his head. He knew he would never see something so beautiful and amazing again. Robbie opened his eyes as the feeling of feathers on his skin weakened. When it stopped, he looked at Bandit and said,

"Well, boy, I think that was the last time we will feel that again here in the flowers." He took a deep breath and looked down at his friend. He knelt down and Bandit moved in on him. "Regardless of what happens tonight, I want you to know that I love you and always will. We will play together tomorrow, I promise. Whether it's here in the yard or in heaven, we will play tomorrow. Now let's go play this game for the last time. Let's end this." Bandit barked and Robbie hugged him. Bandit licked his face until it was a slippery mess. Robbie stood and walked toward the house, wiping his face. How he loved Bandit.

***

Back at the house, they headed back up the stairs. Bandit felt a difference in the air, though, and he didn't like. Not one bit.

Upstairs, the lights were off, which didn't bother Bandit, but Robbie wasn't sure how he would be able to see Dale. Dale would be able to slip in and out of the shadows with little detection. *Do what I do and be ready to call on our help*, Bandit instructed. So they walked in the room where Robbie slept to battle Dale in his deadly game.

***

Dale couldn't believe that Ben was able to not only stop his attack on the two little brats, but he turned it against him, causing him to give up that round. Dale knew he had to strike back, but he also knew he needed to rebuild his energy levels. Demolishing the door, blowing out all the windows, and then levitating the fragments to use them as a missile attack had drained him. He had thought he would have won the game with that devastating move. He thought he would be ripping their souls out of their dying bodies right now. *Damn Ben! Damn that boy for calling on me! Damn me for not preparing for it!*

He sat in the room he murdered Bill in, recouping and regrouping, conspiring and formulating. As soon as he was refreshed, this game would end. *The boy got lucky that time. I won't let that happen again.* Then he cleared his mind, and Dale fell into a trance-like state, praying for power, praying for wisdom, but not praying to the holy. He was seeking help from the unholy. He was asking the devil for a little advice in the matter of Robbie and his companion. Dale began to smile. He liked what he got as an answer to his prayer.

***

"Robbie, Robbie, where are you, baby? Are you upstairs, sweetie?" Robbie's mother's voice sounded through the house.

Oh, no! What is she doing here? I asked her to stay away! She is going to get hurt here, buddy. Dale will hurt her to get to me. He will use her fear to win, Robbie exclaimed to Bandit, with dread heavy in his voice.

Easy. Stay calm. Something doesn't feel right, Bandit thought back to him.

Uneasy steps on the stairs made their way higher and higher, closer and closer to the danger zone of the bedroom. *Your fear for your mother could hurt us all. You must suppress your fear,* Bandit interjected as a shadow became visible at the end of the hallway.

"Robbie? Are you in the bedroom, honey? I am here for you. I wanted you to know you are not alone in this. I love you. Where are you? It's dark up here. I can't see much," his mother called out.

"Mom, I asked you not to come back here for a reason. You have put us all in greater danger. Please leave. I know you love me and I love you very much, but you just have to leave before Dale comes back," Robbie pleaded in a calm and direct manner.

His mother's shape broke the light coming from the open window. She stopped and said, "I just couldn't stay away."

Bandit hunched his body and a growled at her in displeasure.

"Bandit, knock it off. Mom, please leave. You must understand. I need you to do this for me," Robbie requested again as Bandit growled deeper. "What is it, boy? Is Dale coming? Do you feel him?" Robbie asked in short, quick, quiet words.

Your mom feels different. Not right. Evil, Bandit responded quietly in the back of Robbie's mind.

Robbie was confused. Bandit didn't act like this to those he knew and trusted. But it was his mom standing in front of them, right? He had to be sure before he could move on. Robbie knelt down beside Bandit, put his hand on Bandit's back, and began the prayer his mother had taught him when he was even younger than he was now. "Our Father, who art in heaven, hallowed be thy name."

"Robbie, what are you doing? We don't have time for that now," his mother said.

"Pray with me, Mom," Robbie pleaded, now knowing the truth. His mother would never interrupt the Lord's Prayer. "Thy Kingdom come, thy will be done on earth as it is in

Heaven. Give us this day our daily bread." Robbie prayed louder and prouder as he went. "And forgive us our debts, as we forgive our debtors."

"Nooo!" his mother screamed. Now there was a power behind her voice. There was deepness to it. "Stop it now!"

"No," Robbie responded firmly. "And lead us not into temptation, but deliver us from evil."

"You will be delivered to evil. I will take your soul and hand it directly to the devil!" Dale bellowed from where his mother once stood.

"For thine is the kingdom, and the power, and the glory, forever. Amen." Robbie finished his prayer and called for John. He figured Dale would be mad and feel cornered and would want to strike back, so he wanted to be ready.

The house shook violently under Robbie's feet. He stood as tall as he could, without emotion, staring at Dale with his cool blue eyes. Bandit stood firm as well. Head up, chest out, defying the dark power being used on the house to cause it to convulse and sway on its foundation. The wind blew hard through the window frame.

Dale stood tall with his long neck bent backward, his legs spread, so that his feet were slightly outside of his shoulders. His arms rose in a V above his head, so his body formed an X. He then slowly brought his head forward, and his eyes burned with fire and he exhaled smoke. Dale opened his mouth wide, as if yawning, and his belly swelled right in front of his two combatants. His belly grew and grew until it looked as if it would burst open. Then Dale threw up the first snake, then the next. One after another, snakes poured out onto to the floor.

Rattlesnakes, copperheads, cobras, asps, pythons, and cottonmouths crawled on the floor, forming a circle around

Robbie and Bandit. They hissed and struck at them from only a couple feet away. Dale spit out the last slithering reptile and smiled the smile of a new mother, crossed with the arrogance of a bully who is bigger and stronger than his victim. Of course, bullies usually do pick on those who are smaller and weaker, but for every bully there is someone bigger and stronger.

"Brave, brave souls. The two of you are brave indeed. That is why we want your souls so badly. We want the brave, the strong, the kind, the holy, the loving. Those are the souls that taste so good to us, juicy and flavorful. I am giddy with excitement just thinking of my future meals," Dale said. Then he licked his lips with his own snake of a tongue.

"Your tricks don't scare us," Robbie blankly said.

Dale squinted his eyes and snarled his lip in aggravation, as he was insulted. "*Tricks? Tricks!* There are no *tricks* here, you dumb little boy. I am no magician. I am *evil*. I am the devil's worker. Alive or dead, I do his will. I can summon and command the evil of all creatures with ease. Do not mock me, child, for it will be the last thing you do."

"You command nothing. You're a puppet on strings being controlled by the devil. You have no free will and no right to decide on things yourself. You are the child being tutored by the teacher. I'm here because I wish to stand against you with my best friend. He is here because he chose to play your game with me; to beat you, to destroy you. To send you to your devil for eternity so you can't hurt anyone again. To stop the evil once and for all," Robbie replied with conviction.

Dale roared with hatred and disgust. He closed his eyes and began to whistle a tune. The snakes stopped writhing around and fell into a trance. They moved liked pendulums, facing the two enemies, swaying side to side. Empty eyes, mouths opened, fangs ready to penetrate the skin of their target. Dale opened his eyes and drew out the last note for several seconds, then abruptly cut it off. The snakes coiled back to strike, and it began to snow inside the room. The snow fell harder and harder, and within seconds the floor was covered with an inch of frosty snow and the snakes lay frozen in their attack positions, even though Robbie and Bandit didn't feel a change in temperature. Then the snakes and the snow were sucked out the window as quickly as they had appeared from Dale's mouth.

Dale stepped forward and reached for Bandit. Bandit bit at his hand, but found no firm substance to grab. Robbie screamed at Dale and rushed toward him, arms up and out to push him over. Robbie found nothing solid to push and fell through Dale, like falling through a cloud. Dale laughed as he grabbed Bandit by the neck and began to squeeze harder and harder. Bandit struggled against him but could not free himself from Dale's grasp. Robbie stood quickly and stepped into Dale's aura. He felt Dale lose just a bit of strength as he entered his body. Dale maintained his hold on Bandit's neck, and Robbie could see that Bandit was fading. He began to think of the stars and the heavens lit up at night. He thought of his love for his mother, he thought of his love for Bandit, he thought of the flower patch, and he thought of God and Jesus. Dale weakened with each thought, and finally John appeared behind Bandit, who had almost stopped breathing completely. John reached out for Dale and grabbed him by the neck and squeezed. While Robbie and Bandit could not affect Dale's spirit, John could, and he continued to choke Dale until he let go of Bandit. Bandit fell to the ground and Robbie stepped out of Dale and rushed over to him.

Dale swung at John, hitting him repeatedly until he broke his grip on Dale's throat. Dale growled and clenched his fists tightly. "John! Why would you try to defeat me now? You had your chance and you couldn't even save your family, let alone yourself. Why would think you could do it now? I shall destroy your soul as I once did your body. You *fool*."

"I know I cannot win one of your games, Dale, but these two can, and if I can help them my family will be able to finally rest," John said as he charged at Dale. The two spirits clashed. Fire erupted from Dale and John was sent backward against the wall. John attacked again and was repelled yet again. Dale laughed and teased John. Dale motioned for him to try again and John did just that.

John was only attempting to divert Dale's attention away from Robbie while he tended to Bandit. Robbie looked around the floor and saw the cross his mother had given him. He moved toward it on his hands and knees, picked it up, kissed it, and yelled, "With the glory of God, I command you to leave!" And he thrust the cross into Dale again.

Dale had subdued John's essence and was tearing his soul away from him when he heard Robbie yell. He turned to look at him as the cross hit him in the head, stuck inside him. Dale's fire was doused by the good of the cross, and he lost his strength due to the love and faith that was wrapped around the tiny cross.

John moved away from Dale and toward Robbie and Bandit. John touched Bandit and transferred all his energy into the dog. As he did this, John faded from the loss of strength until Bandit had been revived and he was but a shimmer in the room. John nodded to Robbie and then was gone from the room.

Dale shook violently as he shrieked and wailed from the pain of goodness. He glared at Robbie and then disappeared. Robbie scampered over to where Dale had been but found no cross left behind. He looked at Bandit and said, "We need to go to Mom's room now!" The two headed to the opposite end of the hall and entered the bedroom. Robbie ran over to the wall by the glassless window and reached up to grab his new weapon: a silver cross his mother had since she was a little girl.

THE CROSS

In the hills of North Carolina, Mary's uncles lived in old wood homes. Not log homes or even cabins—the houses were made of three-inch thick wood slats pieced together and nailed to the frame. Wood stoves and fireplaces were used for heat. There was no electricity or even running water. Life was easy and simple for these people. Uncle Clayton and Uncle Quincy lived at opposite ends of the mountain. Quincy lived at the top and Clayton lived at the bottom of the mountain.

On a trip to see her uncles with her family, Quincy asked Mary to take a walk with him and Clayton. Mary eagerly agreed and set off with her loving uncles. After walking for a while, Clayton stopped and nodded to Quincy. "Mary, sweetie, you need to be still and listen to what we have to say. It is very important, for it is a message from God Himself," Quincy started. Mary looked from one man to the other with a questioning and bewildered look. She was a religious girl and loved the Lord whole-heartedly.

"Child, the Lord spoke to me and Uncle Quincy just last night. This was no dream. We sat on the front porch, chewing tobacco and drinking coffee, watching nature play in front of us, when the Lord spoke to us both. He said we were to give you a gift, a powerful offering from the Creator. He said that the power inside it could only be used once and it could not be used by you, but by one who will stand strong for your family. You are to keep it safe and never attempt to discover the energy it holds. When the time is right, your loved one will know what to do with it." Quincy spoke evenly and seriously.

The two men looked at each other, then Clayton handed Mary a wood box. Beautiful carvings decorated the outside of the box. Crosses, angels, and rays of the sun through the clouds made up the more prominent markings. She looked at Clayton and he nodded at her to open the box. They had not dared open a gift from God that was not intended for them, and they were curious of its contents. Mary looked down at the box that was a bit bigger than a shoebox and heavier as well. She sat it on a fallen tree and carefully opened the lid. Her eyes grew large as the present inside showed itself, sitting on a soft white satin pillow that had pretty lace edges. She reached in and lightly ran her first three fingers along the cool, smooth surface. She smiled and caught her breath that had eluded her for a few seconds. "It's absolutely beautiful," she said with wonder.

"You need to keep it safe and never lose it, Mary. The Lord would not have given such a gift half-heartedly. There is a purpose for that, and only time will show us what that is. Close the lid now, child, and never speak of its origins. We shall tell Thomas it was a gift given to us by the church and we decided it was for you. This altogether is not untrue." Clayton spoke in awe of the Lord's work.

Mary kept her gift through the years to come and when she bought her new home, with her new husband, and started her new life, she retrieved the box and opened it for the first time since that day in the mountains with her uncles. She thought of what they said and the love she felt from them and the box. A gift from God, they had said. The creator of all things had chosen a gift for her to be used one day by one she loved. She removed the silver cross and hung it on the wall.

The day had come for it to be used by one she loved, a loved one that was a part of her. The powerful present from the heavens.

CHECKMATE

DALE SCREAMED AS he was punished for his failures. Razor blades to his soul, lashings from barbed wire, and burns from a fire that never went out. He apologized over and over again as he quivered from the pain scorching and piercing his body. He was not the biggest and strongest bully on the block, especially this block. Demons laughed as he was whipped and torn apart by his punisher. Then the pain stopped and so did the laughing. He was freed from the telepathic hold that had bound him to the wall. He stood breathing heavily as his wounds healed. Within minutes he was whole again, strong, and ready to end this damn game. He had never met an opponent who was able to counteract his attacks as easily as this boy and his dog. His nightmarish dream from ages ago had finally come to him and he hated it. He hated them like no other.

The voice of his punisher sounded from all around him. "If you fail me again, I will personally see to your torment each and every minute for eternity, or until your soul gives in to the pain and dissipates to nothingness. Then you will be cast to the tombs of hell. Either way, I will be done with you and your bumbling around."

"I have never failed you before, and I will not fail you now, my lord." Dale spoke to the chamber of tortured souls.

"Silence! You have failed me more times than you know, and I will not accept it again. I will only allow you to continue this game of yours once more, due to the amount of souls you have provided me. Do not think that leniency is a sign of affection. You mean less to me than that boy. He, at least, has heart. You used to have heart. You used to have a blackened, empty, bottomless pit of a heart, and now you have become fragile and unclear on your goals and objectives. You had better find your course and provide me this boy's soul or you will pay severely. Is that understood!" The demonic voice boomed through the chambers and halls of his hell.

"Yes, master! Yes!" Dale bowed before his presence.

"Go!" commanded the unholy being.

***

"This is it, boy. I don't think we can take too much more of this. We will fight it out to the end, but Dale keeps leaving and reviving his powers. We can't keep this up forever. We have to finish him off this time. We have to win now. It's the fourth quarter, fourth and goal, and we are at the one yard line, down by five. How I wish we had John Riggins to run it for us." Robbie laughed. As much as he liked the Diesel, Robbie knew in this particular game. Ole Riggo would probably run the other way.

"Stephen. Anibelle. Bill. We need you. We have to finish this now. Please come." As he finished his request, Dale began to storm up the stairs. He took one step at a time, pounding, driving his heels into each step. The wind picked up outside, causing a heavy and hot air to circle the room. A light shone in through both the open window in the room and at the end of the hallway. A darkened grayish light filled the upstairs. This battle would be won with the loser looking into the eyes of the winner.

A hand fell onto Robbie's shoulder and he turned quickly to see the owner. There behind him was Bill, smiling at him. "You have done very well, young man. Now let us assist you in this finale." From behind Bill stepped Stephen, Anibelle, Michael, James, Ben, John, and Elizabeth. All fixed Robbie and Bandit with a smile and a nod, telling him it was their turn to play for a while.

Robbie held the cross with his right hand and put his other hand on Bandit's head and sighed. The cavalry had arrived. Poor Custer. He would have liked this feeling.

The seven spirits stepped in front of Robbie and awaited Dale's entrance into the room. When he arrived, Robbie swore he heard a bell.

Dale brimmed with malice and contempt as he looked at his old contestants. "Get out of the way! I want the boy! Move now, you feeble beings. You can't expect to win against me. I have the powers of the underworld in my corner."

"We have powers too, Dale. We have the holiness on our side, and the boy is not yours to have," Bill said to his old friend.

"I once told you there would come a day when you would pay for the torture and heinous acts you have committed. That one day the Lord would send a soul to defeat you in your game. That one day your soul would burn in hell for eternity. Well, Dale, you son of Satan, today is that day. Today there is one who has the strength to beat you, one who has the power to call upon his friends to help him, one who has the love of the Lord behind him, to send you to your tormented eternal grounds. We have come to help and to watch your soul be vanquished from these grounds forever." Stephen slowly and deliberately spoke.

"You betrayed the trust of my family. We took you in. We fed you, we housed and clothed you. Then you turned on us. You sucker punched us. You killed us, but you didn't take our love for each other and that is what has kept us strong, waiting all these years to take you down. You will now pay for all the pain you have caused." John spoke plainly.

Dale was fuming. He was shaking with anger. He pointed to the group and said, "I will make you all pay for your interference. If you leave now, I will leave you alone. Give me the boy, and you may all go about your ways. If you choose to play with me, our games will be pain, torture, and agony. Games which I know well. Now choose!"

The seven entities chuckled in unison then sprung onto Dale. The move was so swift that Dale was not able to prepare a defense. The group took turns attacking. Early on, the group had the clear advantage. They had Dale surrounded and he seemed to be losing his strength quickly, then one by one he was able to use his telepathic power to push them away or even throw them back. Once he was able to stand free from the onslaught, he raised his hands above his head and spread his fingers to the sky. Fires escaped his fingertips and he shot this fire at his assailants, knocking them backwards and draining them of their energy. As he moved his hand around the room disposing of the band, Bandit shot forward and jumped into Dale's chest, mouth open and teeth bared.

Bandit snapped his jaws shut as if he was trying to snap Dale in half. This time he knew he would only connect with air. He hoped to break up some of Dale's energy, and it worked. As Bandit passed through Dale, Bandit drained him of enough power that the fire ceased exploding from his fingertips.

Dale bent forward as if hit by a mighty blow, and Bandit moved cautiously back to Robbie, never taking his eyes off the dark man. Elizabeth and Anibelle wasted no time and moved in on Dale. They reached into Dale numerous times, trying to get a grip on his cancerous soul. Dale was losing power by the second and was unable to keep them from penetrating him, but he had just enough reserved to fend them off from the essence of his soul.

Robbie stepped forward with Bandit by his side and watched as his friends wore Dale out. All they had to do now was grab his soul and pull it free from his aura.

Then, with a thunderous boom, the entire house shifted and the floor in the hallway split into a volcano of fire and steam. Robbie's friends halted their attack in surprised terror. Robbie looked into the hallway and his heart sunk. *So close. We were so close to winning and ending this.*

"Enough of this. I warned you, Dale. I warned that if you failed me again, I would see to it that your torture be my new hobby." A voice boomed from the burning hole in the floor.

"I have not yet lost. I am still playing. I am still in this game!" Dale shouted back at his master.

"No, you have lost!" A being with the head of a cobra, the horns of a bull, and the wings of a bat floated up out of the fire. The being appeared to have male qualities for legs, arms, and mid-section. Once completely out of the hole, the devil stood nearly eight feet tall and fire consumed the edges of his being. Hatred and malevolence emanated from him so strongly they could almost see it. He pointed to Dale and levitated him off the floor and slowly walked into the room.

Dale screamed and fought against the hold that bound him, but even at full strength, which he was almost depleted of, he could not have saved himself. "NO! NO! I DID SO MUCH FOR YOU! ALL IN YOUR NAME! NO, PLEASE FORGIVE ME!" Dale cried out.

The devil placed his hands on Dale's chest. Then the snake mouth opened and its tongue reached in between his hands and down into Dale's chest. Dale lay there, still, suspended in the air. He was numb with fear. The tongue began to work around like a hand inside a box, looking for the object which it desires.

Robbie stood back by his bed, holding the cross in front of him with both hands. As the creature from the fire stuck his tongue into Dale's chest, Bandit said with his mind, *We must attack now, while it is preoccupied. We can win now, I feel it.*

With that, the souls of Dale's victims launched into a full frontal attack of the thing in front of them. However, this creature would not be defeated so quickly and easily. The power coming from it never wavered as it held all of them in place, feet away from their target.

Robbie took a step forward, then another, as Bandit followed suit. The snake head looked at them while its tongue continued to pull Dale's soul free. Robbie stopped and told Bandit to let him finish his task. "Better to face one powerful being than two. If we attack and Dale's soul is allowed to reenter his aura, he may feel the need to help his master to garner some sympathy."

So the two stopped and watched Dale's struggling soul be torn from its place and slowly be drawn into the mouth of the snake. Dale's body hung limply in the air then dissipated.

The snake head turned to the group and viciously bellowed, "Now I shall do the same to each of you, one at a time, so the next soul will see what awaits them, and so you, boy, will know what fate meets you in the end."

Robbie laughed a bit nervously and said, "The power of GOD is in this room. The power of LOVE is in this room. The power of FRIENDSHIP is in this room. WE HAVE THAT POWER! I will not let you hurt anyone else here. WE ARE NOT AFRAID TO PLAY THE END GAME WITH YOU!!"

A haunting laugh escaped the snake head. As it laughed, the house began to shake again, this time so intensely that the walls cracked and the dressers fell over. Water erupted from the faucets, and the floors cracked and split open, which allowed more flames from hell to seep through. The wind blew so strongly that Robbie had to widen his stance and bend slightly to avoid being blown over. "This is POWER, boy. You know nothing of the POWER I can pull forth at will. I am the *essence* of everything you fear. You and your dog cannot defeat me. I will live forever."

"Not here you won't!" Robbie screamed, and he jumped at the devil creature with the cross out in front of him. Bandit reacted at the same instant, sensing his friend's intentions.

The devil lost his grip of the souls as he reacted to the boy's advance, startled that anyone would dare to attack him. He never considered this an option. John and Bill moved instinctively toward the horned snake as Robbie landed on him cross first. "With the POWER OF GOD!" Robbie exclaimed as the cross burned deep down into the devil's flesh... Flesh!

The arms from the snake creature grabbed the boy and flung him hard against the wall, nearly knocking him out. Bandit arrived just as Robbie flew from its hands. With the snake man's attention on Robbie, Bandit jumped upwards with an explosion from the muscles in his hind legs. Bandit opened his mouth and bared his sharp teeth, intending on tearing away flesh from his enemy. As he reached the snake's neck he thought to the evil being, *Now you feel my pain!* Bandit sunk his teeth deep into the neck of the dark creature. Bandit held his grip and squeezed with every muscle in his body as he hung down the front of the demon, clawing at the body, trying to inflict as much damage as possible. Yellow and green pus began to roll down Bandit's mouth from the wound he was creating with his razor teeth.

The devil's snake head shook wildly to rid itself of the beast attached to it. The devil's hands pounded on the dog's back and head. In a last ditch effort, the devil raised his hands to his sides and came inward as hard as he could. There were a series of cracking sounds, and Bandit yelped as he let his death grip relax and he fell to the floor, gasping hard to catch a single breath of air. The devil looked down and kicked Bandit, sending him across the room and against the same wall where Robbie lay, regrouping his energy and will to fight.

"NOOOOO!" Robbie screamed as Bandit rebounded off the wall and landed at his feet. Robbie dropped to his knees and caringly touched Bandit, who was still fighting for air, but with each gasp, Bandit was capable of less and less effort. Tears filled Robbie's eyes. Only a friend who is losing a friend knows the pain Robbie experienced at that moment. But there was also anger, a rage inside him he had never felt before. He stood, head hung down, and turned to see Bill and John attacking the creature from hell.

"You killed my friend. You killed my best friend in the whole world!" Robbie deeply growled. He breathed in heavily then heard a voice deeply but softly inside his head.

Anger and hatred are the fuel for the devil. Don't give in to your feelings, my son. Battle him with love. You are full of love. Allow that to spill over onto the creature before you.

Robbie calmed himself and thought for just a second, and then said, holding the cross in front of his face, "By the power of GOD and all the angels in heaven, I command you to leave this house. I command you to leave now!" And he stepped closer.

Bill and John felt a break in the power of the evil man and sensed fear creeping into him. They backed off to give Robbie the chance to meet him one on one, as GOD's child of love. They walked over to the others and they then walked over to Bandit.

"You foolish boy! You stand behind a symbol of weakness! I am the only power here!" the devil yelled forcefully.

The wind outside began to howl as it blew harder and harder, snapping branches from trees. The house grumbled as it began to tear apart from the strain of supporting the weight of the power being dispersed by both players.

"You stand for weakness. You stand for wrong. I stand for love. I stand for friends. I stand here, against you, for GOD." He took another step forward. The cross began to shimmy in his hands as a light dimly formed.

The devil snake heard his words and saw the light and felt a pain of fear strike him. The boy was a formidable opponent after all. Maybe he was too quick to judge Dale's inability to dispose of the nuisance. Perhaps. The snake's eyes fixed on Robbie's, and it began to sway from side to side. "You are afraid. You want to give in. You are tired of fighting. You want your friend better."

Robbie answered quickly, unfazed from the attempt to play with his mind. "You speak what you feel inside. You are afraid. You want this to be over. You wish your only friend was still here, but you destroyed him. GOD has granted me a freedom from fear of you. Now I will end your reign here." Robbie stepped forward yet again. Now only four feet from the snake's nose, he removed one hand from the cross, held it up high to the ceiling, and spoke. "Lord, pour your energy through me. Pour your love into me so that I may push this evil man back to the hell he came from. Seal him there so he can no longer curse this place." The light from the cross became blinding.

The devil squinted then rose to the ceiling and roared. Fire escaped his eyes and mouth. He rushed toward the boy and slammed into the barrier that had been placed around him by the Lord. The contact of the two forces created such an explosion of energy the house split from the foundation and the roof fell into the attic, just above their heads.

The devil cursed as it bounced off the wall from its run-in with goodness. Robbie, however, took the opportunity to finish the game. He took two quick steps, leaped, and landed on the devil as it landed from hitting the wall. Robbie regained a two-handed grip on the cross and exclaimed, "In the name of the Father...the Son...and the Holy Ghost... AMEN!" He drove the pulsing cross down into the neck wound which Bandit had created. As the cross dug deeper into the devil's soul, Robbie was thrown back from the percussion of the detonation of all that was evil and all that was good inside the creature. The walls ripped like paper and the house rocked hard from side to side, like a ship in a hurricane. Robbie lay motionless on the floor as the house began to fall down around him.

The devil spasmed on the floor as his soul was ripped apart. His legs changed form and his arms melted into his

The Game Evil Plays

body. He glanced over at the boy on the floor, then over to the group standing by the dog...the dog. The dog was staring at him, watching him. If he made an attempt to snag the boy, the dog would die defending him. The serpent didn't have that kind of time, or power, now. He had to go now. He hissed loudly and slithered to the break in the hallway floor. As he reentered hell, a bell sounded loud and clear.

Bandit strode over to Robbie and licked at his face, but there was no response. The walls were crumbling and the ceiling wouldn't exist for long. The floor wouldn't be able to support them for much longer either. Bandit lowered his head and grabbed the front of Robbie's shirt and began to drag him out of the room. He stopped for a glance to the group now standing by the wall. They were smiling and waving to him. "Tell your friend we said we love him. Thank you for everything the two of you did for our loved ones and us. We shall forever be grateful. We love you, brave Bandit."

I will tell him, and I know he would say you're welcome. Thank you for your help. Enjoy your peace. Enjoy heaven, Bandit responded in their minds. The group slowly faded until the room was clear of all souls.

Bandit continued to drag Robbie out of the room and down the hallway. He got to the top of the stairs and prayed he wouldn't lose his grip going down, which he didn't. Once at the bottom, he loosened his jaws to give them a rest. The muscles were beginning to cramp. Just then a ceiling brace fell and crashed through the stairs, five steps from where the two friends were. Bandit barked at the house, then gripped Robbie's shirt again and tugged on him until Bandit got him moving backward once more. As they made their way into the dining room, the supports for the ceiling in the living room gave way and the upstairs smashed on to the floor.

Bandit looked up and knew he had very little time to save both of them. Then his butt and tail banged into the door. OH, NO, Bandit thought. How was he ever going to get the door open? He was capable of a lot of things but opening closed doors was not one of them.

"Come, young soldier. Bring your friend outside now." A young female voice spoke from somewhere in the house and the door opened wide. Bandit tugged and tugged. His muscles were cramping and every movement felt like he was being electrocuted. He couldn't stop, though; he had to battle through it. Bandit reached deep for more power and suddenly felt a surge of energy flow through him, like the times he and Robbie stood in the flower patch. He pulled Robbie easily across the sidewalk and down into the front yard with his newfound strength.

Bandit let go off Robbie's shirt carefully and looked up at the house as it collapsed to the ground in a dusty, wood-exploding, stone-tumbling heap.

Bandit looked to the right and saw the young and pretty Becca waving to him. She stopped waving long enough to blow him a kiss and then waved goodbye.

"Easy, boy, easy."

Bandit snapped his head to the right and saw Troy. Troy was the guy up the road who owned the store Robbie liked. Troy was approaching Bandit cautiously, but he kept moving in. Bandit dropped his head and growled. Too much had happened to lose his friend now.

"OK, Bandit. OK, boy. Good boy. That's good to watch Rob like that, but I just want to see if he's OK." Troy pleaded to check on Rob and stepped closer, with his hands out and down so Bandit could see he wasn't hiding anything. Troy liked the boy a lot. When he had bought the old country store, Robbie came up to meet him and his family and they bonded quickly. Troy didn't like calling him Robbie so he kept it at Rob, and Rob seemed to like that. Troy, however, did not like Bandit. Oh, Bandit was a good dog and Rob spoke very highly of him, but Bandit scared Troy, as Bandit did to most people.

Bandit stepped back a few feet to give Troy room so he could check on him. Troy placed his fingers on Robbie's neck and picked up his pulse immediately. It felt strong. With Rob breathing well, he stood and put his hand out to Bandit. Bandit walked to it and sniffed it. He also searched Troy's mind and found nothing evil in his mind or his heart, so Bandit licked his hand. Troy patted the top of Bandit's head. "Good boy. You saved his life, big guy. That was the craziest storm I ever saw," Troy stated as Robbie began to move and moan.

Troy is here. Be careful what you say, Bandit thought, reaching out to Rob's mind. He picked that name up from Troy's mind and he liked it.

"Rob? Rob, are you OK, buddy? Can you hear me?" Troy asked.

"Hmmm, yeah. I'm OK, I guess," Robbie answered. He was groggy from his head to his toes. "Where's Bandit? Is he OK?" he asked Troy.

"Right here, buddy, he's right here," Troy assured him.

"What happened, Troy? Do you know?" Robbie slyly asked to find out what Troy had seen.

"Bad storm, buddy. Looked like a finger of God touched the ground right on your house and blew it apart. Tornado, lightning, fire, thunder, explosions, Rob, it was just crazy. You two are lucky to be alive. Bandit pulled you from the house just before it collapsed. Your mom stopped by the store before they left earlier and asked me to call her if anything seemed wrong, so I called her when I saw the tornado touch down on the house. She's on her way, Rob. She should be here any minute, actually."

Bandit moved to his friend and nuzzled up against his face. "Thank you, boy. Thank you so very much! I love you!" Robbie hugged his friend. While they hugged, Robbie reached into Bandit's mind and looked at his memories to see what happened after he was knocked out.

Wait a minute, Robbie said, alarmed. *I could never do that before. We could talk like this, yes. But I just looked into your memories. I actually touched your mind,* Robbie thought, amazed.

Looks like we just got closer, Bandit replied.

Robbie turned, looked at Troy, concentrated on his mind, and tried to peek inside. Suddenly, Robbie was exposed to all of Troy's thoughts, his memories, and his feelings. He also sensed that Troy was good, not evil. Robbie was flooded with these images so fast that he fell back against the ground. Bandit barked. *Yes, I felt it all too and could see the same things you could.* Bandit sighed. *I hope you can control this, because we don't need to have everyone's mind crashed into us just because you look at them.*

I will work on it. Trust me, I don't want to see everything everyone is thinking, buddy, Robbie insisted.

As Robbie sat patting Bandit, a car came down the driveway. "Looks like Mommy's here," Robbie said, pointing to the car.

CPSIA information can be obtained at www.ICGtesting.com
Printed in the USA
BVOW04s0254220114

342651BV00001B/27/P

9 781628 572810